TARTARUS VARIANT

Kurt James

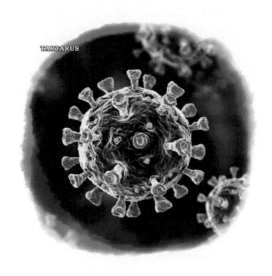

DEDICATION:
To Irene for all your help with making this book a
reality.

KURT JAMES

KURT JAMES

Disclaimer:

This is a work of fiction. Names, characters, businesses, places, events and incidents are either the products of the author's imagination or used in a fictitious manner. Any resemblance to actual persons, living or dead, or actual events is purely coincidental.

TARTARUS VARIANT

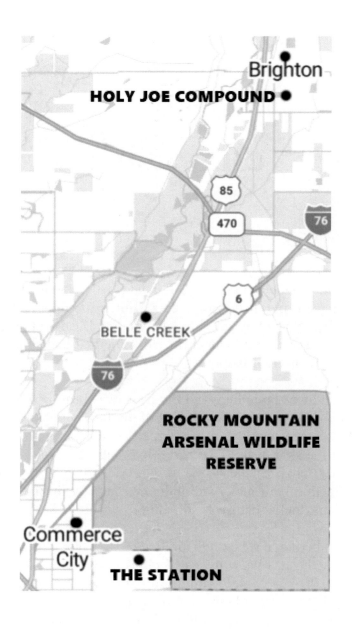

CHAPTER 1

My eyes snapped open, and if I had been standing it would have staggered me, it was now dark with the night - really dark. The day had slipped away. How many hours I had laid here I had no idea. Had it been a Gunner, or Holy Joe that had shot me? Or maybe just a survivor like me?

My head was pounding, and my heart was beating a drum as I reached up and touched the left side of my face and then higher up the bullet graze just above my ear. My face was numb and the blood on the side of my face had dried, but the wound itself was wet to my touch as the lesion still was exuding a discharge of blood. Feeling both lucky and unlucky; unlucky in that someone had shot me, lucky that I was still alive!

Remembering I was south of Brighton, Colorado. Doing the math in my head, I knew it was 14 miles from home, and thinking to myself, "Dixon Mateo, you are a long way from the Station." The "Station" was my home and the safe haven that I had carved out for myself. When the world died, it was the only place I found where, I could lay my head and sleep without the nightmares.

Ripley had her head on my chest as I looked up. And it was a moonless night because of the heavy cloud cover. Seeing me awake, the black German Shepard whimpered quietly as she showed her concern for my well-being. Knowing I needed to reassure her, I tried to reach with my left hand to pet my dog and constant companion. In doing so, I realized I was still holding on to Ella's reins.

Ella was my three-year-old Blue Roan Appaloosa mare. When she saw me stirring, she snorted and used her hoof to paw the ground. It would seem when I had been shot out of the saddle, I had the wherewithal to keep her reins clenched in my hand. Ella moved in closer and dropped her head within inches of my face as if she was seeing for herself, if I was still alive, "Thanks for checking on me girl, I am still alive or at least I think so."

Ella snorted twice, acknowledging my statement, and then lifted her head. Still needing to comfort Ripley, I tried to pet her, but was having difficulty moving my left arm. Focusing on the task, praying and hoping that the plunge from the saddle had broken nothing. Moving my fingers gingerly and then my left arm and then the right one. I was sore as all get out and after moving both my legs, I decided the plummet from the saddle had broken nothing. Although I felt as if I just had the crap kicked out of me. I felt as if Dolph Lundgren as Ivan Drago from Rocky IV had kicked my ass.

Knowing I needed to get moving, I lifted my head to sit up. A wave of dizziness flowed over me. Realizing now was not the time to attempt such a maneuver, I laid my head back down. Letting the spinning lights in my head time to simmer down, I tried to recall what the hell exactly had happened.

It was like having a strobe light in my mind as the memories flashed in and out. I knew someone had shot me, but why? Then a burst of light in my head and the memory of the man yelling and running towards me with a rifle to his shoulder.

Closing my eyes, I concentrated harder as I tried to remember it all. I recalled the man being upset that I had filled my canvas bag with sweet corn. The man in his anger had fired several times at me. One bullet scraped my noggin. I had almost lost my life over a bag of sweet corn! My memories faded to black once again. Had the bullet graze done permanent damage? What happened to the man that shot me? Did he think I was dead? If so, why not take Ella? A horse, especially one that was saddle broke - was valuable?

My thinker had a fog, and I closed my eyes and tried to remember. I had left the Station at dawn to forage. I had plenty of can goods, enough to last the rest of my life. But sometimes I crave something fresh. Before Tartarus, there were farmer's market farms south of Brighton, the ones that grew vegetables and such. At the end of the days of humanity, they had left these farms unattended. Nature and wildlife had overrun the cities and the farms, but sometimes I had gotten lucky finding vegetables such as tomatoes, cabbage, lettuce, onions, and carrots growing wild at the old market farms.

I had seen the field with a few cornstalks in it from previous trips north. Knowing that I could harvest the corn at the end of July. I ventured out from the Station today for some much-needed fresh produce.

Ripley licked my face as if she was telling me it was not safe here and that we needed to get moving. As always, she was spot on.

You never knew when or where a Holy Joe or a Gunner would be patrolling. Once again, what happened to the man that had shot me?

Sitting up, then rolling onto my knees. Blinking fast to keep the spinning lights from taking over my eyesight again, I pushed and with a lot of difficult and painful effort; I gained my feet. I stumbled and had to put my hand out onto the saddle on Ella to keep from falling. Not knowing if I was capable or strong enough to lift my leg into the stirrup. At this moment, I was betting there was no way I could get back in the saddle.

Still trying to gather my thoughts, I looked towards the south where the Station and my sanctuary was and thought the 14 miles to get home was a long way when one was injured and at night. Right now, the darkness was my ally, because without the moon and the city lights which had stopped working long ago, the night was pitch black. Holy Joes and Gunners would have difficulty seeing Ripley, Ella, and me if they were out and about.

The memories of today's events were coming back, still in flashes. To the best of my recollection, I had traveled north, following what used to be highway 85 in between Commerce City and Brighton, Colorado. The paved road had long ago gone into disrepair and littered with cars and trucks that had gotten stranded on the highway from lack of gas. It was mid-morning when I had wandered westward on the road that brought me to the field of corn.

I already had the duffel bag of corn tied to the saddle, when I saw the man running towards me. They always say you will never hear the crack of the rifle that fired the bullet that kills you. At first, it felt as if I had been elbowed in the head—hard. Then the throbbing of the searing heat of the bullet that made the deep furrow along my scalp, all before I heard the report of the rifle.

I still could not remember what happened to the man that fired at me. Did I fire back? I felt along the saddle and located my rifle scabbard and felt the butt of my Henry lever-action rifle sticking upwards. It would seem I had not fired my rifle. Then I dashed my hand down to my holster on my right hip. My holster was empty! My Uberti 45-Long Colt revolver was gone!

Looking about, it was so dark that I could not see the ground. Did I fire and then drop the pistol? Had it just slipped out of my holster? I was still dazed and confused from being shot out of the saddle. I did not want to ride back to the Station without the sidearm, in case I ran into the Holy Joes or the Gunners. Bending down, I ran my hand across the ground, hoping to find the revolver. Nothing but dirt and weeds.

Slowly standing up, for fear of passing out from my head wound, I reached out to steady myself against Ella. Using her to balance myself, I worked my way back to my saddlebags. I reached inside and located my Ryobi 18-volt flashlight. I knew the battery was fully charged. Last night at the Station, I had plugged it into the charging port that ran down from the Honda generator and back up solar panels on the roof.

Holding the flashlight, I was reluctant to turn it on. I was in the land of darkness. No city lights, no moonlight, just the ebony of the night. If I turned the battery-operated light on, it would be a beacon that anyone in the vicinity would be able to see. If the Holy Joes or Gunners were out and about, they would come to investigate. Had to find my Uberti pistol, though.

Taking a deep breath, I flicked the button to turn on the flashlight and, as if the bright yellow and green flashlight had a mind of its own, the light immediately fell upon my pistol. Quickly reaching down, I picked it up and holstered it right away. The movement of holstering my weapon had caused the light to move in a sweeping motion, and that is when I saw him. It was the man that had shot at me. I stared at the body for a half-tic of a minute, before my memory returned in a flash.

Looking at the clothing of the dead man, it was obvious he was just a survivor, like me. Not a Holy Joe or a Gunner, just a man who, like me, liked sweet corn. Turning off the flashlight didn't stop me from seeing what I had done. The dead man's image was now burned into my mind. Lowering my head and closing my eyes, the flashes of memory were no longer flashes. Seeing the dead man had jolted my mind back to reality. I had killed him with one shot to the head. The man and I had fired at the same time. His bullet creased my head. My bullet had taken half of his head off; he must have died instantaneously. I had killed this man over a bag of sweet corn; I remembered it now. It was not one of the proudest moments in my life. It was a hell of a thing taken a man's life over something that in the days before Tartarus would have been unthinkable. I took everything this man was, or would ever be, for a bag of corn. This was the world now. A world that death and destruction was the way of life.

Ripley growled almost silently. Then I heard voices in the distance towards the north. Someone had seen my light and was moving in on my position. There were no friendly's out there, only foes. I had to move away from here, get further away into the darkness. The night would hide me for now.

I was going to have to try and get into the saddle. Reaching out once again, I found Ella, and she was standing still, as if she knew that any movement would cause me to fall and not be able to lift myself into the saddle. Grabbing the saddle horn, I concentrated and then focused my strength in lifting my left leg. Feeling some triumph in being able to plant my foot into the stirrup on the first try. Taking a deep breath and using what was left of my strength, I was able to plant my butt into the saddle. The voices to the north were getting closer, and I could finally make out what one of them said. "The light was shining this way, and I heard something! Whoever it was, they are this way."

Not knowing if they were on horseback or not, but I was thankful they apparently did not have any light source, like a flashlight. Reaching down, I patted Ella on the side of her neck and said quietly, "Take us home girl."

Without giving the Appaloosa any spur, I reined her head around to the south and almost noiselessly we sauntered away into the darkness. Ripley was just making enough noise that I could hear, but not see the all-black dog as she took point in front of us.

CHAPTER 2

It was so dark out I had to trust Ella and Ripley that they knew where they were going. An hour after leaving where I had killed the man over the sweet corn, the sun was beginning its daily arc of a sunrise in the east. Another 15 minutes passed, and it had become light enough I could see for a mile or so in every direction. Pulling back on Ella's reins, I brought her to a stop. I saw no one, no wildlife, nothing was moving. No one was following us. We were alone on the shoulder of what used to be highway 85.

There were several cars, pickups, and one semi-tractor trailer abandoned on this stretch of the highway. Most of them had their doors left open, either from when the vehicle had been first abandoned by the owners or later when the survivors of the Tartarus had rummaged through them looking for anything of value in the world, we now lived in.

My head was still throbbing from the head wound, but I watched the sunrise in all of its red and orange glory. Ripley stopped and came back to watch the sunrise with Ella and me. My first thought while watching the start of a new day was how wonderful and resourceful God been with the creation of nature and sunsets and sunrises.

That line of thought got me thinking of the Holy Joes. Holy Joes was the handle I had given them; they called themselves the Clerics. The Clerics were Christian religious fanatics that saw themselves as soldiers of God. They saw themselves as Crusaders of Christianity, much like those that fought in the medieval Christian religious wars.

The Clerics answered to one man, Joseph Spawn, and Joe Spawn answered only to God; this was according to Joe. The Holy Joes saw Joe Spawn as their savior and thought him to be a prophet. Joe in the early days of the different coronavirus's spreading across the globe, saw desperate folks turning to him and his teachings for the want to understand what was happening to the world. Joe Spawn had charisma and told the masses he had a direct line to God. Joe told those that would become his believers that God spoke through him.

Although I had been brought up in the Lutheran Church with a Christian background, and I was a believer in the God Ole' Mighty. Others, such as I, saw through Joe's bullshit, and realized that Joe was touched, not by God, but by madness.

Joe Spawn and his army of Clerics believed that in 2019, when COVID first started, it was the beginning of the Rapture, the second coming of Jesus Christ from Thessalonians 4:13-17. According to Joe Spawn's thought process that COVID was the beginning of the first phase of the Rapture. As with the many variants of the coronavirus that followed, leading up to the most dominant strain, the Tartarus Variant. Joe believed the Tartarus Variant ended the 1st phase of the Rapture when more that 95% of the world population succumbed to it. The millions and millions of deaths, according to Joe and his Clerics, is that God came for his believers, both living and the dead. It is the Holy Joes' belief that these deaths were the transformation and catching up of all Christians to meet Christ in heaven. Leaving the non-believers behind on the earth.

Joe and his Clerics believe all those left behind are in the 2nd phase of the Rapture. That now is the time of tribulation on earth as foretold in the bible. Joe now believes that he and his God warriors are to cleanse the earth of non-believers.

Joe and his irk believe once they cleanse the earth of non-believers, that Christ will return. This return will be the 2nd coming of Christ. When Christ returns to earth with his church, he will bring the Saints who were raptured in the first phase. Joe's belief is that with Christ's victory with Joe's help over his enemies, and that Christ will reign on the earth for 1,000 years with Joe, his Saints, and his church.

It is my belief that Joe Spawn is insane, and that his followers are just as crazy to be in his cult. Joe Spawn and the Holy Joes were a dangerous and an unpredictable force. Those of us that were not Holy Joes or Gunners were caught in the middle of an undeclared war of sorts. I tried to live my life, and not to draw the attention of either faction. These are scary times and I wondered if mankind is strong enough to survive. It would seem that humanity is on shaky legs and about to go down for the last count. My thought was that nature was just about to inherit the earth. Maybe that is God's plan all along.

Touching my head wound gingerly, I felt the dried blood and knew the wound had quit bleeding. Another wave of pain washed over me and for several seconds - it felt as if lightning had hit me and from my head to my toes I twitched. Gritting my teeth, I waited until the spasm had stopped before I opened my eyes again and looked south towards the Station and home. I needed to get home, where it was safe.

The head wound needed cleaning and Ripley, Ella, and I needed sleep badly. Taking one last look at the rising sun, I reined

Ella south once again and gave her a gentle tap with my spurs. We moved out.

Still following along Highway 85 south, 15 minutes later, I was riding past my old neighborhood of Belle Creek. Belle Creek before Tartarus had been a nice upper middle-class neighborhood with pleasant looking homes with big porches, which gave you the feeling of living in a small-town atmosphere. Most were gone now, including the apartment building I used to live in. Years ago, a fire had started and with no one to man the fire trucks, over 80% of the homes had burnt down to the ground. The commercial buildings in this small neighborhood had been spared since they had been far enough away from the residential homes that the fire had not spread that far. McDonalds, Taco Bell, 7-11 convenience store, and a carwash named Tail Feathers stood abandon with thousands of tumbleweeds stacked up against the broken windows and the brick and steel walls. These businesses had been icons of a simpler time. It all seemed so long ago now.

Suddenly Ripley stopped and looked back at Ella and me and growled. Ripley was giving me warning. I needed to heed it. Giving Ella some spur, I reined her due west towards the old forgotten carwash. Ripley took point and was running towards the building as if she could read my mind.

Tail Feathers' carwash was one of those long tunnel-like carwashes. Before the world crumbled, you would pay the attendant and they would move your car or truck through the various apparatuses. First the rinse, spray foam, spinning brushes, and finally a heavy-duty blow dryer as your vehicle moved forward through them. I remembered loving the smell of bubble gum of the tri-color foam. Reaching the carwash, I could duck down far enough to ride Ella into the building.

Still hurting from the bullet graze, I gingerly climbed down out of the saddle. With my left hand, out against Ella to steady myself, I watched Ripley and focused on my hearing. Doing so, I pulled my lever action Henry rifle from the scabbard and levered a shell into the firing chamber. It wasn't long before I heard the distinct sound of a Humvee engine.

Looking through the murky plexiglass window of the carwash enclosure, is when I saw 3 Gunner Humvees moving slowly down Belle Creek Avenue heading north. A patrol from Cheyenne Mountain near what was left of Colorado Springs.

Wondering... wait... now I hear the "chuff, chuff, chuff" of the whirling blades of the air support helicopter. All Gunner patrols had one armed helicopter as air support. The helicopter is why none of the survivors or the Holy Joes drove any cars or trucks. They were too easily spotted and taken out by a missile from one of the helicopters.

Gunners was the handle I had given them; the Gunners were what was left of the United States government and the military. Here in what was left of Colorado, they were based out of the old NORAD command center in the nuclear blast proof complex at Cheyenne Mountain. Gunners were no longer the good guys.

There were no good guys left anymore in the world. Some survivors that I had spoken with had seen the Gunners snatch other survivors and presumably had taken them back to Cheyenne Mountain for medical testing and experimentation.

Back in 2019, when the original variant of the coronavirus had started, many believed it was a biological weapon that had escaped the Wuhan Institute of Virology in Wuhan in China's Hubei province. Later on, this proved to be the case, and it was determined that the modified virus was engineered not by nature, but by scientists. Playing God had backed fired on humanity.

They also proved that the United States had funded the research to develop this virus. Supposedly, the virus had a unique feature, called the furin cleavage site, and without this feature there is no way it would cause a pandemic. In 2019, there was a reported quote of one virologist that was working on the virus, "I'm going to put horns on horses" and at the end of 2019, a unicorn turns up in Wuhan city. From there, as the world got vaccinated against the virus, it kept mutating and the different variants were getting stronger and even more deadly. Finally, the mutated Tartarus Variant took hold and the world as we knew it succumbed to the engineered virus.

CHAPTER 3

Keeping a close eye on the Gunners, I palmed my Uberti pistol and spun the bean wheel to make sure it was fully loaded in case I had to fight. I would lose, of course, being out manned, outgunned, not to mention they had a helicopter. If they spotted me, with my head wound and the lack of sleep, it would make a quick fight of it. But fight I would. No way in hell would I let them take me alive. None of the survivors that had been taken alive had ever come back from Cheyenne Mountain.

Given the circumstances, Tail Feathers carwash, I realized this was just about the safest spot as we could be in. Big and tall enough to hide Ella from prying eyes of the Humvees and the chopper. Far enough off of what remained of Belle Creek Avenue that they probably wouldn't search unless they saw movement. The plexiglass was dirty and murky enough and with tumbleweeds piled up high enough that I felt they hid us enough not to be seen. Ripley knew not to bark, to draw attention. We just had to wait them out.

Wondering what brought the Gunners this far north, I had not seen a patrol in over 6 months. I was hoping they had become weakened in numbers from the Tartarus Variant and were staying close to Cheyenne Mountain. But here they were. Watching them through the plexiglass, I saw a huge black and white tomcat cross the road and one of the Humvees stopped suddenly and a Gunner stepped out of the vehicle and shot the cat with his rifle. Having killed the cat the Gunner approached it, drawing his buck knife from the sheath on his belt. Stooping over the cat, the Gunner quickly gutted the feline. It would seem this patrol was running short of rations and the tomcat was on the dinner menu tonight.

The Gunner helicopter flew in a circle overhead once and then headed north towards Brighton. I could only hope that the Gunners and the Holy Joes had a run in with each other. It would serve both factions right.

The Humvees followed the helicopter as they continued north on Belle Creek Blvd. I waited another hour after seeing the last of the Gunners, then with some difficulty, I mounted up on Ella. My head was pounding, and I needed to get to the Station and get my head wound cleaned up before any infection set in. A couple of years ago, I had raided a few Walgreens and had a generous supply of antibiotics stashed away. There were another 7 miles to go before I got home to the Station. Hopefully, I could get there with no further delays or incidents along the road.

One last look towards the north, I rode Ella out of the carwash and then headed south away from the Gunners and towards the Station. Ripley, as always, took point. She knew the way and the road home. Following Highway 85 until it merged onto Highway 76. This highway was littered with abandon cars and semi-tractor trailers. Each abandoned vehicle was a ghostly reminder of what the world used to be like. The hustle, bustle, and chaos of driving a busy highway during rush hour was just a memory of how it used to be. Just vehicles rusting away from the summer rains, and frigid cold of winters. Those that had died here on the highway from Tartarus, their remains were long gone to dust as nature, birds, feral dogs, and cats took care of the bodies. A half hour later, still riding south, I rode past the green highway sign proclaiming that I was now entering Commerce City, Colorado.

It was midafternoon by the time I got to 60th Avenue. Reining Ella due east, we rode on past a Grease Monkey, Starbucks, Wendy's, Arby's, and an old Walmart that had been looted in the early days of Tartarus. A couple blocks east of Walmart was one of the older neighborhoods of Commerce City, with some of the houses being built clear back to the 1940s and 1950s. I was an hour away from the Station. The last 48 hours had been rough on Ella, Ripley, and me.

I had killed a man for a bag of sweet corn, which I still had, and was tied off to my saddlebags. My head bore the wound of being shot, and there was a patrol of Gunners north of me. I just needed to get home to the Station.

A couple more blocks eastward, Ripley stopped and pointed due east and the hair on her back stood up. She turned to me and growled. Pulling the Henry rifle from the scabbard, I levered a 45 long colt shell into the chamber. Having done that, I gave Ella some rein and her head and we moved cautiously up so we were standing side by side next to Ripley.

That is when I saw the pack of feral dogs. After Tartarus, almost all domesticated dogs had been left alone when their owners either had died or they had to abandon their former pets when they could no longer care for them. Now the cities were overrun with packs of former domesticated dogs. Each generation of the feral canine packs became wilder as they reverted literarily to a dog-eat-dog world.

With my left hand, I reached back and grabbed my field binoculars from my saddlebag, which brought the dogs into better focus. There were 10 of the wild dogs. Generation after generation of uncontrolled breeding had made them all into mutts. Some were as big as Ripley, which made them a very dangerous obstacle to get around to get home. My luck on this outing had been the shits from the very beginning. I was not in any shape to tangle with a pack of hungry wild dogs.

So far, the dogs had not noticed us. The dogs were distracted and focused on a large oak tree. They were barking and running around the base of the tree. Obviously, they had treed something and were trying to wait whatever was in the tree out so they could feast on it.

Now I refocused the binoculars on the upper branches of the tree. At first, I couldn't see anything, then I saw movement. The dogs had run down a person and had forced them to take refuge in the tree. With a closer look; not just a person. Even from this distance, I could recognize the curvature of a woman.

Shaking my head, knowing the woman would more than likely end up getting killed by the dogs and eaten, or she would die of dehydration sitting in that tree.
Speaking quietly to myself, "Shit, just what I needed."

I couldn't leave her there. I was going to have to try to rescue her.

I watched the pack of dogs for another couple of minutes and decided the big black and brown brute of a dog with the face of a boxer was the alpha male. Hopefully, if I took him out, the others would scatter.

Reaching behind me, I secured my binoculars in the saddlebag. Once again, I checked the loads in my Uberti pistol. Having done that, still holding my Henry rifle, I laid it cross ways on my saddle, ready to do battle if necessary.

My head was drubbing from my head wound and I really was in no condition to battle a pack of wild dogs. But if I left the woman to whatever fate had in store for her, I could never live with myself.

Looking at Ripley, "What do you think, girl? Do we ride out of here, or go rescue the woman in the tree?"

Ripley barked twice and then stood and pointed her nose towards the tree and the wild dogs. The hair stood up on her back, showing she was willing to risk her neck to save the woman.

I leaned forward and rubbed Ella's neck, then I asked her, "How about you, Ella? Are you willing to go to battle over a woman that you don't know?"

Ella snorted twice and stomped her right hoof three times as she nodded her head up and down. Ella, just like Ripley, was willing to risk herself in this rescue attempt. Ripley and Ella made me full of pride of my extended family. The 3 of us could not have survived as long as we had so far without each other.

Not trusting my eyesight with my own injuries, I needed to get closer to have any chance of picking off the leader of the pack. I hoped the dogs would be so focused on the woman in the tree that they would not notice us until I got within range.

"Well, girls, time to move in slowly!"

Tying Ella's reins into a knot, I left them loose so they could ride easily on the back of Ella's neck. Holding my modified Henry rifle, I then gave Ella a little spur. My Blue-Roan Appaloosa with me in the saddle moved forward with Ripley just to the left side of us.

Once I got within 80 yards and feeling comfortable enough that I would be able to hit a dog at that distance. With a soft-spoken command, I said, "Ella, stop."

Once Ella got her feet squared under her, she gave me a stationary platform to fire from. Bringing my rifle slowly to my shoulder, I peered through the Leupold VX-Freedom Scout 1.5-4x28 scope on the rifle and took aim at the dominant male.

Just as I was aiming for the leader, as if given a silent command, all the dogs stopped and turned their heads in our direction. They had just caught our scent.

That few moments of the dogs being motionless gave me the opening I needed, and I slowly squeezed the trigger of the Henry rifle. I missed. The 45-long colt shell went over the head of the alpha dog.

Levering another shell into the chamber, I fired quickly and this time the bullet hit home and the leader of the pack took a tumble when he was hit. Levering another shell into the firing chamber, I took aim at the next biggest dog and fired. That dog, some sort of Husky mix, also took a hard tumble. Just as the Husky went down, the remaining dogs bolted in our direction.

Now that the dogs were running in an all-out effort to reach us, my next 2 shots missed. Keeping count soundlessly in my head, I had fired 5 rounds, meaning I had 10 rounds left in the modified Henry. With 8 dogs left, I needed to make each shot count. With 2 more hurried shots, which missed, my ammo count went to 8 in the rifle, as the wild dogs now were within 40 yards.

Ripley inched forward, ready to take on the pack, as I fired twice more, taking out the white long-haired dog in the lead. As the dog went down, hard in the pack's front, 3 other dogs tumbled as they ran into the dying white long-haired dog. That broke off the attack, as the rest of the still living dogs scattered.

Ripley took point and was keeping a watchful eye on the remaining dogs as I reloaded my rifle, just in case we were not out of danger yet.

The savage pack was now down to 7, and they had split up, with 4 on my right and 3 on my left. About 75 yards away, the ones on my right had run and then stopped and turned towards us. The 3 on my left were closer at about 55 yards, having stopped and turned watching us. They were eyeballing us still but sitting on their rumps as if they were waiting.

I could pick off a few more at this distance but saw no need to waste ammo. I didn't think with their leader's dead, they would take us on again.

Giving Ella some spur, I moved us forward as Ripley watched the regressive dogs on the left and I monitored those on the right.

Riding past the long-haired white dog, from the bleeding visible in the fur, the wild dog took my bullet in its chest in mid-stride. Probably was dead before it quit tumbling.

When Ella, Ripley, and me were 10 yards from the tree, and 30 yards from the dead white dog I heard the remaining 7 in the pack barking as they rushed in on their dead comrade and started tearing it to shreds as they quickly devoured the white dog. Tartarus had really knocked us all, humanity, wildlife, and apparently once domesticated canines back into the behavior of our Stone Age ancestors.

Keeping an eye on the branches of the tree, we moved closer to get a better look at the woman. I rode Ella around the base of the tree several times. Then I laughed. With a glance towards Ripley, I said, "While we were fighting off the dogs saving her butt, she escaped. No hello, no thank you, and not even a kiss my ass. She just took off."

As I was still smiling and then looking up into the tree once more to make sure the woman for sure had disappeared, I heard Ripley growl. Then a voice behind me, a female voice, she said, "I appreciate what you did. I am not sure why you did what you did, but mister I am thankful that you showed up."

Turning Ella to face the voice, my smile faded. The woman with a 2-handed shooting grip was pointing a Beretta APX Centurion semi-auto pistol at me as she stepped out behind a tree on the other side of the street. In a calm voice, "Let me see if I got this straight. I save your ass, and then you point a pistol at me?"

"No offense mister, but with all that dried blood on your face, you really don't look like the friendly type."

Without thinking, I reached up and touched my head wound, which made me grimace from the pain. I laughed, "Yeah, believe me Miss, I feel as bad as I look. You should see the other fellow. Had a run in with a survivor and possible Holy Joe last night."

"Holy Joe?"

"Yes, one of Joe Spawn's lunatic followers, the ones that call themselves the Clerics. I call them the Holy Joes, you know after—Joe. My name, however, is Dixon Mateo."

The woman smiled at me, and my nickname for the Clerics. She said, "The name 'Holy Joe's' fits for sure, and they are lunatics. My name is Alba, Alba Jesse."

"Now Miss Jesse, since we are friends and all, could you please lower that pistol? You are upsetting my dog and my horse. You and I both know you don't have any ammo in that Beretta."

"Now Mr. Mateo, why would you think such a thing?"

My smile got bigger as I replied, "You can call me Dixon, Miss Jesse. If you had ammo in that pistol, you would have started shooting at the dogs when they had you treed."

Alba Jesse said nothing for half a minute, then she smiled and lowered her gun and then smoothly stuck it in the holster that was strapped to her right leg. Another 30 seconds passed when she said, "Yes, ran out of 9mm ammo last week, and every gun store that I have rummaged through since then, all the ammo and guns are gone. And you can call me Alba, if you have a mind to."

Alba was a pretty girl about my age, which was 30 years old. She was small, about 5'4" tall with short brown hair. Her eyes were big and dark brown. Her stance told me, although small in stature, she was powerfully built like an Olympic gymnast back before Tartarus. She was wearing brown leather cowboy boots, tattered blue jeans, and a green hoodie with the Colorado State University logo on the front.

I had not seen a living woman in the flesh in over 5 years, or at least up close. Not sure if it was the loneliness, or that I was just hankering for the sight of a woman, but Alba stirred my blood. Without thinking it through, I said, "Alba, if you want, I can make you a hot meal, and I can give you a couple of boxes of ammo that fits that pea shooter you have."

Alba was running my suggestion through her mind, then she asked, "And Mr. Mateo, what do you expect for this generosity?"

"Hadn't really thought about it before I asked. Not even sure why I asked, other than I had not seen or talked to anyone in the last 5 years that wasn't trying to kill me. Of course, if you want to stay out here with no ammo and a pack of wild dogs roaming the area, that would be your choice. As far as I know, it is still a free country."

Alba's face broke into a grin and she said, "Well, Dixon, since you put it like that, I accept your invitation. Just know I still have my 6-inch buck knife and I know how to use it."

"That Miss Jesse, I have no doubt!"

CHAPTER 4

Ripley decided to make her acquaintance with Alba and walked up to the girl and dropped her head so Alba could pet her. Chuckling out loud, I said, "What the hell Ripley, that girl just pointed a gun at me!"

Alba put her hands on her hips and laughed, then said, "Mister, it was an empty gun!"

Which made me laugh. Alba promptly started rubbing my dog behind the ears, just like she knew from the get-go that was Ripley's favorite spot to be rubbed.

Ripley was enjoying the attention and ignored me. Alba was enjoying it as well; she had a huge smile on her face. The girl with no ammo went from being on the dinner menu for a bunch of feral dogs to having a lapdog in the span of 30 minutes. To say the least, life in the world of Tartarus was unpredictable.

Thinking of the wild dogs, I looked to the west and the remaining 7 dogs were gone. The carcass of the white dog that I had killed was also gone. Either completely devoured or the others had dragged it off for another meal someplace else. As long as they left us alone, I was okay with that.

Sliding my Henry rifle back in the scabbard, I study Alba as she was petting Ripley. She was dirty from being on the road for who knows how long, but she had a presence about her. Ripley, as it would seem, had fallen in love with the girl, and for my dog to do that meant that she was special. She looked up at me and our eyes connected, and I had to look away, because I felt I was staring at her. Her face was so delicate and beautiful. It had been a long time since I had even seen or talked to a woman, let alone gaze at one in the eye. I felt like a young schoolboy pushing a pig-tailed girl in the kiddie swing before Tartarus. Just knowing Alba for the few minutes that I had; her smile, her being here with me, brought me joy and happiness. Knowing, I looked frightful, with my head wound and blood on my face. I almost felt ashamed to be here with her, looking like this.

Alba turned around and headed back to the tree she was hiding behind when we had come to her rescue. Ripley followed her, wagging her tail. Alba retrieved her framed backpack, with an insulated sleeping bag attached to the bottom of the pack. Slipping the pack onto her shoulders, when she asked, "Dixon, it would seem your dog likes me."

"That Alba would be an understatement, if I had ever heard one. She seems to love you."

Alba looked me once again in the eye, "I love dogs, unless of course they are trying to eat me."

We both laughed at that. It felt good to laugh with someone. It had been so long. I could not remember the last time I had laughed so freely.

The sun on the western horizon was above the mountains. I decided we only had about 2 hours of daylight left. It would not behoove us to be out at night with a pack of wild dogs in the area.

Motioning to the east, "We should get moving towards the Station. It will be safe there, and you can even take a hot shower, before I fix us supper."

"Hot shower, supper, and ammo? I have not had a hot shower in more years than I can count. Since my mother died from Tartarus, no one has offered to cook me a meal. Are you for real Dixon Mateo?"

"I think so. But since I got shot in the head last night, I am no longer sure. The Station where I live is a Godsend for sure. I am lucky to have it. You will be safe there, and you will be able to sleep easy. There is plenty of room. You are more than welcome to join me for however long it suits you."

What was wrong with me? I didn't know this woman from squat. I didn't know her story, her life, if she was touched in the head like so many of those that had survived the onslaught of the virus. But looking into those dark brown eyes, none of that matter, I didn't care. All I wanted to do was to take care of this woman.

Alba said nothing about the comment "join me for however long it suits you." My wording must have seemed out of place, or maybe even out of desperation. Which neither was my intent. Hell, I am not even sure why I said what I did. No taking it back now. It was out there. All she said was, "Dixon, how much further is it?"

I pointed down 60th Avenue towards the east and replied, "Not far, maybe a 20-minute walk from here."

Still trying not to stare at the mysterious woman, I gave Ella some spur and her head and we moved out slowly. Alba could match the stride of Ella and Ripley had taken point.

Once we reached the west side of the crossroad of 60th Avenue and Quebec Street, I pulled back gently on Ella's reins, bringing her to a halt. Still sore from being shot out of the saddle last night,

I tentatively dismounted. I placed my hand on the saddle to steady myself once I had my feet on the ground. Moving backwards to the saddlebags, I retrieved my field binoculars.

I tied Ella off to a tree that hovered over an old Regional Transportation Districts bus stop. I then pointed at the bench under the tree that people used to set on while they waited for their bus to come. "Set down and rest. We will be here for about 15 minutes."

Alba did as I suggested, then I did the same. Using the binoculars, I focused in on the large building in the rear and the smaller building in front on the east side of Quebec. There was a large empty field before the parking lot that served both buildings. The field was completely overrun with tumble weeds and prairie dogs.

To the north were even more open fields of what used to be the Rocky Mountain Arsenal wildlife refuge. Prior to the 1990s, the Arsenal was a complex that designed and manufactured chemical weapons to be used in the wars that the United States fought. When chemical weapons were banned by the talking heads in the United Nations, the American government paid to demolish all the buildings at the arsenal. Of course, at the time they contaminated the ground with the chemicals of war and the government spent untold millions cleaning that up. Once that was done, they turned it into a wildlife refuge.

It would seem that man has been trying to destroy humanity since they learned how to make war. It would seem that the scientist at the Wuhan Institute of Virology in Wuhan in China finally did just that when their manufactured virus mutated into the Tartarus Variant.

Alba finally broke my concentration as I was watching the buildings with my binoculars. "Why are we sitting here? What are we waiting on?"

I lowered the field glasses, then pointed across the street and across the field at the larger building. "That Alba is where I live. Had an incident a couple of years ago when a couple of Holy Joes had followed me without me knowing. Now it is my routine to hold up here and survey the area to see if anyone is following me, and or if anyone is lying in wait for me. As you know, not being cautious will get you killed. There is always someone wanting what is yours."

Alba seemed surprised and even said so. "I am surprised you live in such an enormous building. Wouldn't it be hard to defend that building by yourself if needed?"

I turned to face her, "That's the beauty of it, and I don't have to defend it. The smaller building in front was the South Adams County Fire department, which is of no use to me. The larger building in the back was the Commerce City Municipal Building. It housed the courts, building department, and the police station. The police station is in the north end of the building is highly secured. It has heavy duty doors with electronic locks. Anyone who might be curious about the building cannot access that part. I live in the police station. I just call it the Station. Sometimes the best place to hide out is in plain sight."

Alba laughed, "You are telling me you live in a police station? How do the electronic locks work without electricity? How did you gain access if no one else can?"

"That is exactly what I am telling you. I live in the old Commerce City police station. And, I have electricity, or just enough to suit my needs. I have solar panels, wind turbines, and 2 generators. A natural and regular gas generator up on the roof. I can't run the whole building, but I don't want to. Lights draw unwanted attention. I just keep what I need to live supplied with electricity. As for access, I have an electronic key card that unlocks the doors."

Alba still seemed confused. "How do you know how to make all of that work? How did you get an electronic card for the building?"

"I have had the key card way before Tartarus. I used to be head of the building's maintenance. It was my job to keep all the equipment running. So far, I have been able to still keep what I need running to survive."

Scanning the area once more with the field glasses and seeing no movement, I looked at Alba and said, "I think we are in the clear. Are you ready to go see the Station?"

Alba stood up and looked me square in the eyes. "One last question before I go with you. What happened to the 2 Holy Joes that had followed you home here to the Station?"

Not wanting to mince words here. Alba needed to know what I was capable of. So, I told her the truth, "I shot and killed both of them, leaving their bodies in the open field in front of the station for the coyotes to feed on."

CHAPTER 5

With some effort and Alba's help, I was able to mount up into the saddle. With a slight jab of my spurs. Ella and I started across Quebec Avenue. Ripley and Alba matched our stride. Ella knew the road well and could move around the potholes in what was left of the pavement.

There were not as many abandon vehicles on Quebec Street as there had been on highway 85 and Interstate 76. People had fled this neighborhood to places unknown. Remembering those days, it seemed that folks felt the need to flee, even though they had no place to go.

Looking to the north, the sky was turning ugly as a storm was brewing and approaching us at locomotive speed. I could see lightning intermixed within the clouds. For reasons I did not know, nor did the science of it seem to make sense to me, in the aftermath of Tartarus ravaging humanity, nature's fury took hold as if it was God's plan to cleanse the earth. Storms were fierce, be it rain, thunder, wind, dust, snow, lightning, and hail; they seem to be twice as bad as they were before Tartarus. The climate of the earth was changing. Before Tartarus, some believed it was because of man and his pollutants and energy consumption caused the climate to change. Others believed it was a natural ongoing process since the beginning of time. Now, with only 5 percent of the human race still on the planet, no one could claim it was man's doing. Just like the ice ages before humankind walked the earth, the earth and the climate were evolving with man or no man.

The storm looked nasty and was gathering strength and headed our way. It was good that we were so close to the Station and shelter.

We followed 60th Avenue, past the old fire station, and then worked our way to the north end of the parking lot to the entrance of the sally port of the police station. Most of the chain-link fence that used to secure the police car parking lot had succumbed to the ferocity of the storms that flowed through the area.

As I dismounted, Alba notices several security cameras and pointed at them, then said, "Too bad those do not work. They would come in handy if you could see out without having to look out a window or open a door."

"They work. I have the complete security system up and running with monitors and alarms in a room in the basement of the police station."

Alba's face showed some confusion. "Every security camera I have ever seen, you could tell they were on because they had a red light showing they were working."

"Those red lights were a deterrent in the old days to burglars and such, because they could tell they were working. Remember, we are hiding in plain sight here. I disabled all the red lights on the cameras. My thought is if someone came along and saw that the cameras were functional, they would know there was someone in the building and that we had electricity. This way they look non-functional, and hopefully, with the doors being locked, they move on."

Monitoring the storm sweeping down on us, I walked up to the hidden keypad to the right of the sally port door. I punched in the code and the door rose. Once the door was high enough to admit Ella, I took her reins and walked her in, with Alba and Ripley right behind us. Alba looked around, and then said, "I will be damned. I was wondering where you kept your horse, you turned this garage or whatever it was into a barn. This is all pretty amazing."

Once we were all inside of the sally port, I took one last look to the north at the fast-approaching storm. We could hear the thunder just a second or two after the lightning flashes. Just as I punched in the code to lower the door the hair stood straight up on my arms, and we were blinded by the flash of light when a bolt of lightning hit the ground in the open field to the west not more than 100 yards away.

It started as a slow roll across the heavens and then ended with a clap of thunder so loud and boisterous that it shook the sally port door. The lights flickered and the storm's shenanigans visibly shook Alba. With her voice unsure, she stated, "That was close."

The lights flickered twice more, then they stayed on. Looking at the roof of the sally port as if it was possible to see the storm raging outside, I said, "Pretty sure lightning hit the building. It happens more and more frequently than it has in years past."

Alba's eyes got big and said, "Lightning hit the building? You don't seem too concerned about it."

A smile crossed my face. "Not too concerned. The lightning rods installed on the roof would have directed the charge to the ground. I assure you we are safe."

Still listening to the storm rage outside; first things first, and that was always taking care of Ella and Ripley. I fed the mare some grain and hay pellets I had taken from the Stockyards Ranch Supply store. Ripley got a can of dog food that had been taken from the same feed store. I had an old freezer that no longer worked and had taken the door off it and laid it on its back that I used as a water tank for Ella. Turning on a single-handle faucet just above it, I filled the freezer with enough water to give Ella a drink. Then filled Ripley's water bowl.

Alba was once again astonished. "You have running water? I didn't think anyone had running water anymore."

Turning to face her, "I do. I even have running hot water for a shower."

Alba shook her head in disbelief and then smiled. "How is all that possible?"

"Not more than a mile from here was the South Adams County water district. The water that supplied most of the county came from there. The water is still there, ready to be pumped up out of the ground and into a tank up on the hill that stores 200 thousand gallons. Once a year, I start up the gas generator and run the pumps and refill the water tank. After Tartarus, I shut off all the principal lines in the city that I could except the one running here. So, for now, I have running water. There will come a time when the underground pipes wear out or burst, or the pumps fail. Then I will have to do something different: keeping this place supplied with water and electricity is a full-time job for me. But I look at it, as, what the hell else do I have to do?"

Alba nodded her head in understanding while saying, "Yes, nowadays surviving is a full-time job."

Using my electronic key, I opened the door to the police station for Alba, Ripley, and myself. The upper floors had no lights, and I explained that to Alba. I had turned off all the electricity to everything on the main floor, and the 2nd floor. Did this for 2 reasons, one to conserve my batteries where the electricity was stored that the solar panels and the wind turbines generated. But also, to prevent any light shining through the windows. The only place I had electricity for lights was in the basement that had no windows to the outside world.

Once we were on the first floor, we could hear the distinctive clatter of hail, which had been riding in the storm. Alba and I went to a heavy-duty window facing north. They had laced the window inside the glass with steel wire to make it almost impenetrable and tough enough to withstand the hailstorm that was now beating against it.

Darkness had fallen as the hailstorm ravaged the field to the north of the Station. On what was left of the paved road in between the wildlife refuge and the Station was now littered with bouncing ¾ hail. It was a surreal sight each time the lightning lit up the sky with blue and orange thunderbolts.

All at once, I felt exhausted as I watched the storm. Being shot, and the night of no sleep, not to mention rescuing Alba from the pack of wild dogs, had worn me out. Weakness had made me stumble and Alba reached out and touched my arm to steady me. Once Alba Jesse touched me, it felt as if she had hit me with a cattle prod. Turning, I looked into her eyes and I knew she felt it as well. It was the physical touch of another human that we both had craved. We both turned our eyes quickly from each other as we tried to come to terms with being physically close to each other. I had forgotten what it felt to be close to a woman. It felt... wonderful. The only thought that crossed my mind was how thankful I was that she was here.

I tried not to be obvious in my attraction to Alba. I said, "I will show you the living quarters downstairs. There are three rooms set up with beds. They used to be sleeping rooms for the police to use and rest in during emergencies. The old break room has a fully functional kitchen and now is set up like an apartment. There is also a fully equipped workout room. The best part, Alba, is that the old police locker rooms, both the men's and the women's, have showers with hot water."

After showing Alba where the women's locker room was, I then showed her how the shower functioned. I then mentioned that there were women's clothes still in the lockers that had been left behind. If she was so inclined to try them on for something different to wear, she was free to do so.

Ripley had followed Alba into the locker room, and it would seem now that the girls had grown accustomed to each other, they would stick together. Somehow it seemed fitting, and I was okay with that.

A few minutes later, I stepped into my shower, and the steam generated by the almost scorching water was a relief to my aching muscles as the events of the last 24 hours had fatigued my body.

There was a seat in the shower, and I sat down and lowered my head to let the water rush over me. Using a bar of peppermint soap, I cleansed my head wound. In doing so, it bled again from where I had been shot. Knowing I needed to get every bit of dirt out of the wound, I vigorously kept washing it with the soap.

Once I thought my head wound was washed thoroughly, I lowered my head again and let the hot water wash over me as my mind raced with thoughts about the girl in the locker room next door. I could not get my mind off of Alba Jesse and my reaction to her. What was it about the mysterious girl that I so readily with little thought and knowing nothing about her invited her into my home? Why did I give her the keys to my kingdom in this land of damnation? It was so unlike me. One look at her and I was smitten, like a young boy before Tartarus. Rarely ever do I do anything on an impulse, but I did just that when I invited Alba to stay here. What was done was—done. No changing that now.

Deciding my head wound and the rest of my body were as clean as they were going to get, I turned off the water, then stepped out into the locker room and used a towel to dry off. Then I used a washcloth to dab my head wound, and the bleeding seemed to have stopped. I stepped up to the wall hung sink. Using the washcloth, I wiped off the condensations that had built up on the mirror from the steam generated from the shower. Looking at my reflection, and what looked back at me was a haggard, if not a crazy-looking mountain man type, that I used to see in the movies back in the day. My dark brown eyes seemed haunted. I was 30 years old and was 6'2" tall and was lean, weighing in at about 190 pounds. My hair was dark and long enough that it touched my shoulders. My beard was dark with a sprinkling of grey in it. Before Tartarus, women thought I was handsome. My reflection told me I had lost my edge in that department.

Remembering when Alba touched me and the jolt I felt. I could not help but wonder if she thought I was good-looking. Thinking of Alba made me nervous and contented. A weird combination of emotions that made me want to avoid her and or be with her. Nothing in my thoughts was making any type of sense.

Thoughts of Alba in the women's locker room stirred my blood. There was no doubt I was attracted to her. The problem with human attraction is not knowing if they will return it. I did not want to make a fool of myself, but I am sure in the next day or so, that I would do just that. It had been so long that I had any interaction with anyone other than Ella and Ripley.

The more I thought about it, knowing over the last couple of years, I had died a little each day, becoming hollow inside. But the second I saw Alba pointing her pistol at me, and the way she was looking at me, I knew. She was going to be the death of me - or she was going to be the one who finally brought me back to life.

My hair was a mess, and using a hairbrush, I combed my hair into some a sort of civilized look; I decided that a haircut and a shave would do me wonders about how I felt about myself. Any grooming that was required would have to wait until after a hot meal and some much-needed sleep. The exhaustion of the last 24 hours had really kicked my ass.

I dressed in a clean pair of Wrangler blue jeans, a Denver Broncos hoodie, and white socks. I felt a tad better.

Once I felt presentable, I stepped into the hallway. I could still hear the shower running in the women's locker room. Wasting water was not a good thing in the world we now lived, but I let Alba enjoy her first hot shower - in who knows how long. It made me smile, knowing I could give her that.

CHAPTER 6

While Alba was in the shower, I walked past the armory and the surveillance room on the way to the pantry. The pantry had been a food storage room in the police station basement for emergency rations for the city of Commerce City. Since Tartarus, it was now my personal pantry of dry goods. It was a large room of about 1500 square feet. It had rows of shelves extending all the way to the ceiling with many canned foods, and freeze-dried rations. All of which had a 25-year shelf life written on the packages. Not sure how long it had been here prior to me occupying the Station, but for now all of it was still good. More than I could ever eat in a lifetime.

After grabbing 2 packages of "Travelers Stew," I headed back to the surveillance room and sat down and took several minutes to scan the 10 security monitors that showed the outside of the building. The storm had ceased, with no more lightning to light up the sky. The overhead clouds created an eerie shadow from the moonlight that was trying to peek through. What light there was -

was not much, but just enough that it showed the hail had been abundant and it had created dams in the roadway in between the Station and the wildlife refuge to the north. Watching the wildlife refuge monitor for a full minute, I saw no movement other than the swaying of the tall grass from a slight wind. Scanning the monitors to the east, there was enough light to see the soccer stadium that had been named Dick's Sporting Goods Park. It was where the Colorado Rapids, the former professional soccer team, used to play. The stadium had fallen into disrepair and one of its distinctive arches had fallen in and crushed the main gate entrance. There was no movement to the east. Looking to the monitors that faced south and, once again, no movement. Out of the corner of my eye, I caught a movement on the monitor facing west. Something in the distance was moving south along the edge of the parking lot and across the field. Concentrating, I saw it again, and realized it was a couple of coyotes. Nothing to be alarmed about.

I looked in on the monitors a couple of times a day. Although the building was just about as secure as anything left in this world, I did not want to be taken by surprise. My best defense to the best of my knowledge, was that no one knew I was here. The Holy Joes that did were now dead.

Standing up fast, a wave of dizziness swept over me and a headache that had been a dull throb suddenly became very piercing, as if someone had stabbed me in my temple. It was at this moment I could hear ringing in my ears. I stumbled, then grabbed the wall to steady myself for several minutes until I no longer felt faint. The killer headache and the ringing in my ears persisted. I was totally exhausted and needed sleep. The thought now crossed my mind that the bullet glancing off my noggin had given me a concussion. Once I had my bearings again and was confident, I would not pass out, I headed for the break room.

With the packages of freeze-dried stew clutched in my hands, I wandered to the break room area where the electric stove was. Putting a pot of water on to boil water first for the sweet corn that

I almost died harvesting. Then another pot of water on the stove to heat water to use for the freeze-dried stew. As I watched the water boil, another wave of faintness swept over me, and my right hand started to shake. Then I heard a voice behind me. "Dixon, what do you think?"

Slowly turning towards the voice, I saw Alba as she stood in the doorway of the break room. Her smile was as big as all outdoors. She was wearing a blue floral casual summer dress that did nothing to hide her tight and womanly body beneath it. Once she saw me looking at her, she spun slowly in a circle, giving me a good look as she said, "I found it in one of the lockers after I took my shower. What do you think?"

Even though my head was pounding, and my ears were ringing, I was able to say, "Oh my God, you are absolutely beautiful!"

As Alba did another twirl, my legs twitched, and I stumbled. Alba's smile faded and a look of concern crossed over her face when she said, "Dixon, are you okay?"

Even my own words sounded slurred to me when I said, "Yes, I am fine." I started to fall as my vision faltered and my mind faded to black.

~

My eyes snapped open, and my mind tried to focus. There was a light filtering in from the open door. Open door? Where was I? Closed my eyes to let the floaters that were spinning in front of my eyes, time to find a home and quit spinning. After a full minute, I slowly opened my eyes again and thankfully, the floaters were now gone. Turning my head slowly since my neck was stiff and sore, I realized I was in my bed. I felt as if Walker, Texas Ranger had dropped kicked me in the head. My mind was sluggishly coming into focus as it concentrated on what happened. My memory, or was it, started coming back slowly? Once again, I was in sort of a fog. I had been making dinner and I must have passed out right after talking to Alba. Alba? I remembered now.

Alba was standing in the doorway wearing a dress. An exquisite summer dress. Or did I hallucinate that? Was Alba even real, or have I finally gone bonkers? If she was real, where was Alba now?

Slowly rolling my legs over onto the floor, I lowered my head into my hands to ease the pounding headache I was experiencing. As soon as my feet hit the floor, Ripley laid her head onto the blanket on my lap and whimpered slightly. That made me smile. Apparently, Ripley was as real as I remembered. Reaching out to pet Ripley behind her ear, I said, "Thanks for caring for me, girl. Not sure how long I have been out. I bet you and Ella are starving. I better get you guys some chow and water."

"Ripley and Ella just ate and have been watered. Had to feed Ripley in here with you. She would not leave your side. That dog sure loves you."

The voice came from the open doorway, and I raised my head and there was Alba standing there, wearing blue gym shorts and a white wife beater T-shirt. Laughing, I said, "Oh my God, you are real! I was wondering if I had just dreamed about you. Or maybe my mind had finally snapped. I would have sworn you were wearing a dress, though."

Alba laughed, "I was, but when you saw me in it, you passed out. I always thought I had nice legs, but apparently not, if you keeled over at the sight of them. Besides, that was 2 days ago."

"What? I have been out cold for 2 days?"

"Getting shot in the head must have given you a concussion. Imagine that? But not exactly out cold. You would tell me how pretty I was when I was spoon feeding you Lipton instant chicken noodle soup. Did you know you have about 4000 packets of Lipton chicken noodle soup?"

I rolled my eyes, then chuckled, "I did know that whoever was in charge of this shelter must have really liked Lipton chicken noodle soup. They stocked the pantry with enough for the apocalypse. And guess what, Alba—here we are enjoying the fruits of that obsession."

Alba's smile was as big as I remembered. "Dixon, get dressed and I will whip us up a freeze-dried supper of spaghetti and meat sauce."

"Actually, I am starving, and my belly is rolling from hunger. That soup you fed me kept me alive, but I need something more."

I stood up quickly and the blanket that had been on my lap dropped to the floor. That is when I realized I had been sleeping totally naked.

Alba raised her eyebrows as I swiftly snatched up the blanket. I know my face was a couple of shades redder than it had ever been before. What the hell, I just exposed myself to the only woman I have spoken to in the last 5 years. I lowered my gaze, since I could no longer look her in the eye. Speaking in an embarrassed tone of voice, "Alba, I apologize. I did not know I was naked. In my defense, I was just shot in the head, for pity's sake."

By the look on Alba's face and the smile, she was relishing my awkwardness when she said, "Nothing I haven't seen already, Mr. Mateo. Who do you think drug your butt in here and undressed you? Now put some clothes on and come get some supper."

Alba turned and headed down the hallway towards the break room as I quickly did the math in my head. Shaking my head and feeling a tad foolish. It took roughly 48 hours to make a fool of myself.

Ripley even had her head turned sideways, as if she was trying to decipher out how I could look so stupid in such a short time. I looked straight at Ripley and raised my arms and turned my palms up and said, "Jeez, Ripley, whose side are you on, anyway? The least you could have done, was give me a heads up about me being naked."

Finding a pair of boxer shorts, and as I was putting them on, I thought, not only did I expose myself to Alba, apparently, I kept telling her how pretty she was in my delirious state. The more I rolled that thought around in my thinker - at least I didn't lie to her.

CHAPTER 7

The next 2 weeks of life at the Station almost seemed—normal. Having Alba here with me seemed as right as rain. She was a wonderful, hardworking, not to mention that she was easy on the eyes. Since the world died, I had felt no joy whatsoever. I realized I had just been making the motions of going through life, but none of it was enjoyable. Until Alba came into my life. It was as if we had always been together. Just in our short time with each other, it was as if we could read each other's mind. Even Ella and Ripley seemed happier. Each morning and night, I checked the security monitors, and I could view the world outside of the walls of the Station. I knew just beyond the reaches of the cameras' sight that life on the outside was death, destruction, radicals, and the decay of what used to be. Here within the walls, Alba, Ella, Ripley, and I had created a safe haven.

Every 2 days, Ella and Ripley got plenty of exercise as Alba and I took them across the road to the north to the wildlife refuge. Alba had never ridden a horse, and I taught her to ride Ella. Alba, athletic as she was, took to riding Ella as if she had been on a horse back her entire life. Ripley would chase after them as if her tail had been caught on fire. It was a joyful time, being able to experience this. Ella and Ripley accepted Alba into our lives as if she had always been there. It was hard now for me to imagine life without Alba.

After Tartarus and before Alba, I had looted an extensive DVD and CD collection from the surrounding stores, like Walmart. Since most of the world had no electricity, the old streaming services such as Amazon Prime, Netflix, and Hulu died when the world perished. Music and storytelling had been reset to an earlier time. Nothing new was out there, no new music, no new television show, or new movies. The only thing that remained were the physical copies of the older than Tartarus entertainment. Finding these DVDs and CDs were like gold to me. Since I had electricity, I had also looted the very best in a stereo, sound bars, and a combination DVD and CD player. It probably was the only thing that kept me sane in the last 5 or so years.

My Grandfather and father loved country music from the 1990s such as Tim McGraw, Faith Hill, Garth Brooks, Clint Black, Alan Jackson, and Toby Keith. My grandfather had a special love of what he termed "outlaw country" from even an earlier time, such as the 1970s and 1980s, with such performers such as Waylon Jennings, Willie Nelson, Charlie Daniels, and Jessi Colter. I grew up listening to this old and forgotten tunes of the now long dead singers and songwriters and learned to love them. Alba had a similar background to music. Her grandparents and parents and she also had a soft spot in her heart for the same type of music.

It was not unusual for us to crank up the music and dance with each other as we prepared our meals in the break room. Every time we danced; I could feel the sparks fly between us. When the world died, I had buried my feelings to survive. My heart had become cold and calculating. But when I held Alba close to me to slow dance, those long-lost feelings came flooding back. This woman, who came out of nowhere, made me feel again as she and my feelings for her stirred my blood. Feelings that had been locked away for so long, I was unsure how to deal with them. We would look into each other's eyes, and I wondered if she felt the same way I did. Did she know I desired her like no other? I wanted to kiss this woman, but the fear of rejection held my hand and my lips. At night when I was alone in my room, and Alba was alone in her room, the frustration of having her so close, but yet so far, made me feel so alone until I saw her again the next morning. Had I fallen in love with Alba? Or was it just lust? Or was it both? Believe me when I say at night all alone in my darkened room, I pondered the meaning of all of this. What my mind and thoughts kept coming back to was — did I even know what love was? Did I know how to show it? I loved having Alba Jesse here with me, but frankly, it was driving me crazy.

At the start of the 3rd week that Alba had been staying at the Station we fell into our normal routine before bed in watching a movie on the DVD player. Alba found an old black and white film with a man and a woman staring into each other's eyes on the cover photo. She said, "Oh my Dixon, don't they look so in love?"

Alba tossed the DVD carrier over to me and I read the description of the movie. "Rick Blaine (Humphrey Bogart), who owns a nightclub in Casablanca, discovers his old flame Ilsa (Ingrid Bergman) is in town with her husband, Victor Laszlo (Paul Henreid). Laszlo is a famed rebel, and with Germans on his tail, Ilsa knows Rick can help them get out of the country." Looking at the photo again, I assumed the man was Humphrey Bogart, and the woman was Ingrid Bergman. Tossing the movie back over to Alba as she stood in front of the DVD player and television. Once she caught it, I said, "Never heard of the movie or this Bogart fella."

Alba once again looked at the photo of the 2 stars, and I could tell she wanted to watch it, so I said, "If you want to watch it, I will watch it with you."

Alba's face lit up, as she slid the round disc into the DVD player. She then bounced back over to the couch and set down beside me. Ripley found her usual spot on the floor in front of the television and promptly fell asleep.

We both became enchanted by the old black and white movie as it played out across the television screen. Although the movie was ancient, it was one of the best movies I had ever seen. The gist of the movie was it truly was a love story of not 2 people, but 3. The movie centers on World War 2. Rick Blaine (Bogart) and Ilsa Lund (Bergman) met and fell in love in Paris, France. Just before the Germans conquer and occupy Paris, Rick and Ilsa decide to meet at the train station and flee the advancing German army. While waiting at the train station, Rick receives a brief note from Ilsa that she cannot join him. Rick is heartbroken and ends up in Casablanca Morocco as the owner of Rick's Café. Casablanca has become the final destination to flee the German horde to America. Problem is, you have to have letters of transport to catch a flight out. Rick has 2 of these letters. One-night Ilsa shows up in Casablanca with her husband Victor, who was and had been a rebel against the German political machine. Victor Laszlo (Henreid) desperately needs 2 letters of transport for himself and Ilsa to get to America. The Germans want to arrest Lazlo. Ilsa does not know that Rick's Café is owned by her former lover, Rick Blaine. Rick and Ilsa's reunion is obviously strained. The husband Lazlo is clueless about their former love for each other. Finally, Rick finds out that in Paris, when he had fallen in love with Ilsa, she had believed her husband to be dead in a German concentration camp. She found out right before they were supposed to flee Paris that her husband was not only alive but had escaped. That is why she sent the note and stood Rick up at the train station. Rick still loves Ilsa, Lazlo loves Ilsa, and Ilsa loves both men. Lazlo and Ilsa know Rick has 2 letters of transport and is the only one that can help them escape. Ilsa promises to stay with Rick if he helps Lazlo escape by giving him a letter of transport. Rick agrees, but at the last minute at the airport, Rick kills a German trying to arrest Lazlo. In a tearful, but fantastic scene at the end of the movie, Rick gives the 2 letters of transport to Lazlo and Ilsa just before they fly out to freedom in America.

Rick stays behind in Casablanca to face what may come. Great movie, great love story of uncontrollable circumstances.

During the movie, there were a couple of quotes spoken that seem to hit home with Alba and me. Once the words were spoken on the television screen, Alba and I looked at each other, knowing somehow, they were meant for the 2 of us.

When Rick and Ilsa were in Paris as the Germans were advancing, Ilsa said, "With the whole world crumbling, we pick this time to fall in love."

Later, when Ilsa and her husband show up at Rick's Café in Casablanca, Rick says, "Of all the gin joints, in all the towns, in all the world, she walks into mine."

After the movie, Alba and I retreated to our separate bedrooms, and I thought about the movie. How even in the gravest and most dangerous times, that love somehow triumphs! In the end, that no matter what happens, that loving someone is really what life is all about.

There was a light knock on my bedroom door, then the door opened, and Alba stood there dressed only in a white towel — nothing more. For a few seconds, all we did was look at each other, then Alba said, "We live here in a precarious time. Maybe it is the end of times. We do not know what the next day brings. I am not going to wait any longer, Mr. Mateo." At that moment, she let the towel fall away, exposing the beauty of her that had been hiding beneath it. As she slowly moved towards my bed, Alba repeated another quote that Ilsa had said in the movie Casablanca, "Kiss me as if it were the last time."

CHAPTER 8

The summer months passed quickly at the Station. Now we were at the end of September waiting for the cold and snow to blow in, with winter approaching soon. The lightning and thunderstorms had continued, most with sizable hail. One storm at the end of August did considerable damage to the roof and windows that were in an adjacent wing of the building when baseball size hail took out most to the windows facing north. I could repair the roof of the wing that housed the old police station with supplies left over in the maintenance department. In fear of running out of material, I did not repair any of the roof over the other wing of the building. I needed to fix and secure the roof over Alba's and my head.

Since my trip to Brighton, we had seen no one. No Gunners, no Holy Joes, and no other survivors such as ourselves. It was as if the world had reset, and Alba and I were the new Adam and Eve. As for the Tartarus Variant, Alba and I did not know if it still existed in nature. We spoke many of the nights on the subject. Even though we had watched all of our friends and family wither away and die from the respiratory illness, Alba and I never came down with the sickness. We did not know if we were just lucky enough not to catch it or if we had a natural immunity from it. Since the world died and science along with it, we would probably never know.

Alba, Ella, Ripley, and I stayed close to home, with no need to forage for food, weapons, or ammunition. Since we had control of the armory here, we were blessed with an assortment of weapons and a large stock of ammunition. The only ammo we used up was once a week. We honed our shooting skills at the indoor shooting range that the police officers had used. It was a short range of 30 yards, great for handguns. Our supply of emergency food rations seemed endless. During the summer and early fall, we were able to let Ella graze on the wild grass at the wildlife refuge. But I feared I would not have enough hay pellets and grain to get through the winter months. Last time I was at the abandoned Stockyards Ranch Supply store, there was a large supply of hay pellets and grain. Hopefully, those ranch supplies were still there. It would take many trips by horseback to gather enough supplies to last throughout the winter. I would have to ride Ella there, then load her up with duffel bags of supplies and walk her back to the Station. Probably take more than a week to get stocked up. So, we were going to have to start soon before the snow started to fall.

Stockyards Ranch Supply store was just over 3 miles away and since Alba or I would have to walk besides Ella, it was my thought it would take one hour to get there, and an hour to load up with supplies, and one hour to return to unload. I was hoping to make 2 trips a day until we had enough supplies for Ella for the winter.

As per our routine, Alba and I armed ourselves to venture outside of the Station. While in the sally port converted into a barn, and after saddling Ella and tying off some empty duffel bags behind the saddle, we checked our weapons. Alba had her fully loaded 9 mm Beretta semi-auto pistol holstered and strapped to her right leg. The rifle scabbard riding on Ella housed the Henry lever-action 45 long-colt saddle rifle. I was armed with my Uberti

45 long-colt revolver that was in my holster on my right hip. Deciding we would need more modern firepower in case we ran into trouble, I grabbed from the armory an Mk 14 Enhanced Battle Rifle (EBR) which was an American military selective fire battle rifle chambered for the 7.62×51mm NATO cartridge. No scope, just iron sights. The Mk 14 had one fully loaded 20-round detachable box magazine inserted. Deciding more was better, I grabbed 5 extra fully loaded magazines.

Checking the security cameras to make sure there was no one on the outside of the Station. Seeing there was none, I opened the garage door of the sally port to the outside world. It was a beautiful day that greeted us. We could see the snow-capped Rocky Mountains to the west. There was a slight breeze, and the temperature was about 60 degrees. The sky was forever blue on this cloudless day. It was going to be good to get out and about for the day.

Once we moved Ella and Ripley outside, we decided Alba would ride and Ripley and I would walk. I strapped the Mk 14 Enhanced Battle Rifle over my shoulder. Ripley took point as we moved out.

On the way to the feed store, we passed the tree that Alba had climbed to escape the pack of wild dogs. Luckily, today so far, we did not see any of the feral dogs or anything of that sort.

It was good to stretch our legs, and we made the feed store in exactly one hour. A smile crossed my face, because all the hay pellets and sacks of grain were still there. A little less, maybe because of the rats that scurried around, but still, plenty of supplies to get Ella through the winter. After loading up with no problems, it took us an hour to get back to the station. With Alba and me both working hard, it only took us 20 minutes to unload and store the supplies until we were back out and, on the road, again.

We were about a ¼ of a mile from the feed store when Ripley suddenly stopped and crouched down low, still facing in the direction of the feed store. Alba had been riding Ella, and I quickly grabbed the reins and brought the Blue Roan Appaloosa to a halt. Alba said, "Dixon, what's the matter?"

I quickly removed the battle rifle from my shoulder. I then pointed towards Ripley, and quietly said, "When she crouches like that, there is something up ahead that shouldn't be there. Ripley is warning us that something is amiss."

Alba dismounted and grabbed the Henry rifle from the saddle scabbard. She then quickly levered a shell into the firing chamber, before she said, "What do we do now?"

"We need to check out what is bothering Ripley. Ella needs that feed from the store. It might be nothing. But, before we do that, do you remember the code to the doors at the Station, in case something happens to me?"

Alba, still holding onto Ella's reins, she said, "Dixon, I do, but whatever happens is going to happen to all of us. Ripley, Ella, you, and me are in this all together."

"Well, Alba, that attitude is one of the reasons I love you!"

That stopped Alba in her tracks. She turned to look at me. "What did you just say?"

A smile spread over my face, then I said, "I didn't stutter, yes you got attitude. Then I said I love you."

Alba chuckled slightly, then said, "Mister, attitude is all I got. That is not what I was talking about, though. You take this moment of possible danger, to tell me you love me?"

"I did, in case I get killed, and I wanted it out there, so that you would know."

"Dixon Mateo, you are an asshole! You couldn't tell me when we are making love, listening to some country tunes? You had to wait until we were possibly in danger, to tell me you love me?"

"Well yeah! Seemed like as good a time as any."

Alba's, smile went from ear to ear, as she said, "I guess, if I was to hook up with some dipshit in the end of times, it is better to be with one that loves me, just as much as I love him!"

Trying not to laugh out loud, I said, "Dipshit? And you also love me?"

Alba moved in closer and moved her rifle to her left hand, and she stood on her tiptoes. She then took her right hand and pulled on my shirt so that I lowered my head so she could kiss me. After a spell, she quit kissing me, then looked me in the eye, and said, "Yes, my love, you are a dipshit sometimes. But you are my dipshit, and I love you like no other in my life."

Ripley growled in a low tone, bringing Alba and me back to reality. Still making eye contact with the woman I love, "I think you need to keep Ella here while Ripley and I take a look see up ahead."

Alba nodded her head in understanding that Ella would be easier to spot than one man and a dog. Alba took Ella's reins and moved her off the road into some cover of some overgrown trees. Walking up beside Ripley, in a hushed tone, I said, "Let's go, girl. Show me what you already know."

I kept the enhanced battle rifle unslung and in my right hand as Ripley and I moved to the side of the street. Using the abandon cars and trucks as cover, we advanced forward to the feed store.

When we were within a block of the store. Ripley and I stopped, and I took the field glasses from my backpack and used them to survey the store. For the first 30 seconds, nothing seemed out of the ordinary, when finally, I saw a horse's tail swish several times. The building hid the horse, and all I saw was the tail twitching. Moving to the north 75 feet, I found a red Ford F-250 that had seen better days. All 4 tires were now flat, and all the glass was blown out of the door windows and windshield. Now using the pickup's bed as cover for Ripley and me, I used the field glasses again and took another look at the feed store.

There was not one horse, but 3 horses and 3 men. The men were heavily armed and wearing the white collars, like a Catholic priest would have worn in the old days before Tartarus. The Holy Joes were loading up on grain and hay pellets, just as Alba and I had done earlier.

I squatted lower behind the bed of the truck. Looking at Ripley, I said, "Thinking we will cool our heels until they are completely loaded and have started back to their encampment. Not sure it is advisable to tangle with 3 armed Holy Joes. We will wait to load up again once they have left.

Ripley did a low growl. I tried to give her a stern look, but failed at it when I smiled, before saying, "Not like you, girl, to be itching for a fight."

Just as I had spoken the word "fight", there was a loud bark. Then the bark got louder, and a dog went into a frenzy of barking. Quickly I looked over the bed of the truck with the field glasses and sure as shit, the Holy Joes had a dog, which I had not seen earlier. A big muscular dog looked similar to a pit bull. The pit bull was looking directly at me the whole time he was barking. A quick look at Ripley, like she didn't already know, I said, "The Holy Joes got a freakin' dog! That dog knows we are here!"

Ripley turned her head sideways as if to tell me, "That is what I have been trying to tell you!"

Taking another quick gander at the Holy Joes over the top of the bed of the truck. One man made a gesture in our direction as he was talking to the dog. It was obvious he had just told the muscular dog to "sic 'em". The dog wasted no time and bolted in our direction.

CHAPTER 9

The Holy Joe's dog was about halfway in between the feed supply store and Ripley's and my position. The 3 Holy Joes themselves were in a hurry to get mounted. There was no doubt in my mind they would attack our position once their dog had us engaged.

I aimed the enhanced battle rifle, and once I had a clear target in my sights, I slowly squeezed the trigger. The pit bull took the bullet in mid-stride. He took 2 more lunges, and then the Holy Joe's dog stumbled, then collapsed not 20 yards from the Ford F250. The muscular dog was down and out of the fight.

Killing the dog didn't slow the 3 men as they now were mounted on their horses and they had started giving their mounts their spurs, pushing them hard into battle. These Holy Joes must have been experienced horsemen, since they could fire their rifles when their horses were at a full gallop and gaining speed.

The first 3 shells fired by the horsemen thudded into the pickup bed. Then a fourth bullet spun so close to my head, I could hear the whine of the bullet as it flew on by. Taken aim at the man in front, I slowly squeezed the trigger, and he took my bullet dead center of his chest, dropping him from his horse. Once the front rider had dropped from the saddle, his horse veered to the right, colliding with the 2nd and closest rider, causing that Holy Joe's horse to stumble, tossing its rider headfirst into the decaying pavement of the roadway.

The 3rd rider was still charging and firing his rifle as more bullets embedded into the side of the truck. This rider was firing so quickly I had to keep down below the top rim of the truck bed in fear of getting shot in the head again. In just a few seconds, the Holy Joe rider was upon our position. The man seemed to enjoy bringing his horse hard around the old Ford truck, exposing me to him. What the Holy Joe didn't know was I had a dog of my own. Just as the 3rd rider cleared the end of the truck, Ripley went into action and went for his horse. A thought flashed through my mind, "Yes, asshole, I got a dog."

Ripley's attack on the horse was so swift, and the surprise completely put the Holy Joe and the horse into a panic. So much, in fact, the black mare went to bucking and upended its rider, spilling him onto the ground. The Holy Joe's horse was in such disarray from Ripley's unyielding nipping at her flexor tendons on the back of her legs. She bolted right over me, knocking me to the ground. The panicked horse ran me over so hard that I lost my grip on my enhanced battle rifle, which flew about 30 feet away. After the horse collided with me, I slammed my head on the ground, which brought a whole milky way of flashing stars into my eyes. Shaking my head, trying not to pass out; in only a few seconds my eyes cleared, and I could finally see the Holy Joe that Ripley had tumbled from his saddle. The Holy Joe had already gained his feet, and he, like me, had lost his grip on his rifle, but somehow, he had pulled his 10-inch bladed knife from the scabbard on his side. Ripley had now positioned herself in between me and the Holy Joe, protecting me, and was growling something fierce. The Holy Joe was taller than me by a good 4 inches and outweighed me by about 50 pounds. The man was muscular and looked strong. And by the way he was holding the knife, he had experience in knife fights. Still clearing out the cobwebs from being run over by the horse, I finally gained my feet and was facing the Holy Joe. The man looked half-crazed when he smiled, then said, "Gonna carve your dog up first, then I am gonna carve you up, mister. Once that is done, I am going to eat your dog. She looks really tasty."

This Holy Joe might be more experienced in knife fights than me, but the radical zealot had brought a knife to a gunfight. In a practice maneuver, I fast palmed my Uberti revolver and promptly shot the Holy Joe in the throat first, then the 2nd bullet took him right between the eyes. Walking up to the now dead Holy Joe, I said, "Threaten me all you want! But nobody's gonna eat my dog!"

I heard distinctive Ella snort, and I turned around as I was holstering my pistol. There was a look of concern on Alba's face as she dismounted Ella. Once Alba had her feet firmly on the ground and still holding Ella's reins, looking at the dead Holy Joe at my feet, she said, "As soon as I heard gunfire, I hightailed it here as fast as Ella could carry me. I now stand corrected. My man is not a dipshit. He is one badass."

Just as Alba finished talking, Ripley growled, and I heard a movement behind Alba and me. Both of us palmed our pistols and spun around in a 180 at the same time. The 2nd rider apparently had gained his feet after being de-horsed, and was now standing 30 yards away, lifting his rifle in our direction. He never had a chance as both Alba and I both fired killing the Holy Joe. Even before the dead man hit the ground, Alba quickly asked, "How many more are they?"

"I only saw 3, pretty sure there was only 3."

Just at that moment, I heard a horse neighing in the distance, and then the thunder of hooves, and a man's voice yelling to his horse, "Go, go, go!"

It was obvious I had missed a Holy Joe. He must have been hidden further back around the building. Turning my gaze back toward the feed store, I saw a 4th Holy Joe give his horse some spur as he reined his mare around several abandon cars roughly and then started galloping north. I hurriedly retrieved my battle rifle from where it had gotten tossed. The fleeing rider was the focus of my attention. I slowly squeezed off a shot and—promptly missed. Taking aim again, and just as I was getting a bead on the remaining rider, he rode his horse behind an abandoned tractor trailer. After that, I lost sight of him completely.

Alba walked up beside me as we continued to look north in the direction the Holy Joe had disappeared. After several seconds of silence, I looked at Alba and in frustration, I said, "If we could have stopped that one, then the rest of the Holy Joes would not have known what had happened to their patrol. They would not know where this patrol went missing. They could have succumbed to wild dogs or the Gunners anywhere on the trail from here to Brighton. The bad news is now they have a starting point close to our home to be looking to avenge the deaths of their comrades. The good news is, we just gained you a very valuable horse of your own."

I was only able to capture one of the Holy Joes horses, a palomino mustang that the 3rd rider had ridden. The other 2 Holy Joe horses were so skittish. When I tried to herd them, they broke free and bolted back to the north towards Brighton and the Holy Joe encampment. It was just as well. Trying to care for 2 horses was going to be a tough enough chore.

The palomino mustang mare that the 3rd rider had been on was a beauty. She was smaller at 13 hands, and perfect for Alba. The mustang's body was muscular, with a well-defined and narrow chest. Built much like Alba herself, its new owner.

Mustangs are a mix of the Andalusian, Arabian, and Barb horse breeds. European settlers brought mustangs, which originated from Spanish horses to the United States. The word mustang is actually derived from 'mesteno', a Spanish word meaning wild or stray. Over time, some mustangs escaped and became wild. Others were captured and stolen from their owners. If the mustangs were wild, they were then broken to ride by American Indians.

Even though Ripley and the palomino had squared off when the Holy Joe attacked; they both seemed to sense now they were on the same side. After just a few minutes of sniffing and getting to know each other, the palomino lowered her head, as did Ripley, as they playfully lunged at each other. Ella seemed indifferent to the new horse, but Ella was just that way. All in all, it was starting to look as if the new mustang seemed to be happy to be in our family. Alba, now that she knew how to ride, was itching to be on her new horse. Alba looked at me and said, "Dixon, what do you think? Do you think she will let me ride her?"

"Only one way to know. Let's get you on her, so you can take her for a spin."

Since Alba had shorter legs than the previous Holy Joe rider, I had to adjust the stirrups for Alba's legs. As I was doing this, Alba made sure the saddle was still tight and had not loosened up during the time the mustang had gone to bucking when it tossed its rider. After checking the cinch strap and flank billet strap, she picked up the rear skirt of the saddle, and then she said, "Dixon, what do you make of this?"

I had just finished the adjustments on the stirrups, and I walked to the back and looked at what Alba was talking about. Stenciled into the bottom of the skirt was a simple name: Bonita. Waving my thumb, as a hitchhiker would do twice at the Holy Joe on the ground, I said, "I doubt very much if it is that fellow's name. Might be the horse's name, maybe. If it is, that would seem fitting. My Spanish is a tad rusty, but I believe Bonita means 'pretty'. The horse is an exquisite and a pretty mustang, and its new owner is an exquisite and a pretty woman."

Alba smiled as she walked to the front of the horse as she said, "Mr. Mateo, you only say that, because you have not seen a woman in 5 or 6 years."

That made me chuckle. "Miss Jesse, you got a point there. For all I know, with all the remaining women in the world, you might be the ugliest of the bunch. But I highly doubt it. I have seen movies with beautiful women, and I would not trade you for any of them."

Alba, still all smiles, was petting the bridge of the mustang's nose when she looked at me, "Dixon, you are sort of a fancy talker. Guessing that is why I decided to fall in love with you. That, and the fact you are very handsome. Plus, you saved my ass from being torn from limb to limb by a pack of wild dogs."

Alba was talking to me, but without speaking to the mustang, and by the obvious love that she was showing the mustang, it was really the horse she was communicating with. Alba turned her full attention to the mustang and looked her straight in the eye, and in an almost whisper, she said, "What do you say Bonita, do you want to be mine?"

Bonita lifted her head and stepped in one step, then lowered her head behind Alba's back, embracing Alba in a hug. In this insane and dead world that Tartarus had created, that hug between Bonita and Alba was one of the most beautiful things I had ever seen.

Alba was able to get her foot into the stirrup, and in one motion, she could mount and square her cute little butt into the saddle. Holding on to Bonita's reins, she looked at me. Once my woman was safe in the saddle, I said, "Take it easy. You don't know this horse or how she handles. No galloping!"

Alba laughed out loud, then she said, "Let's do it Bonita, let's show this stick in the mud how it is between us!" With that, Alba gave Bonita a little spur and off to the races they went. In six strides, Bonita and Alba were at a full gallop. Alba and Bonita had already bonded, and they rode as if they were born to each other. Watching them together was a rarity in grace, spirit, beauty, and fire. Alba on the mustang signified strength, freedom, and confidence. It was like watching the beauty of the wind. My heart was skipping a beat now and then, not out of fear for my girl, but out of love. How did I get so lucky to have this woman grace my life? I was so in love with Alba Jesse!

CHAPTER 10

For the next week, Alba and me, with the help of Ella and Bonita, moved hay pellets and feed grain from the feed supply store to the Station. Each time we went for another load, we would approach the store with caution, worried about running into a patrol of Holy Joes. There was no doubt in my mind that they would return in force looking for those that were responsible for killing 3 of their members. The key was keeping the location of the Station a secret. Hopefully, in time, the Holy Joes will think we had been drifters and had moved on.

Each time we returned to our home with a full load, we took a different route, and kept an eye on our back trail. Since Ripley's senses of hearing and smell were more in tuned than Alba and mine, she was essential in letting us know if we were being followed. We had been lucky so far, and it was not until the last trip to the feed store that we had any hint of danger. When we were halfway back to the store for the last load of supplies, is when the sky in the north turned black with an impending storm. As was the norm now in this world of Tartarus, the storm's intensity was mushrooming, and the wind was picking up speed.

As the black clouds in the north rolled closer to our position, I looked around and there was no place close to house Ella and Bonita, to keep them out of harm's way of the storm. As both Alba and I study the brewing storm, I said, "We need to forget this last load for now and move south towards the old Walmart on 60th Avenue. The loading docks and garage doors in the rear will give the horse's access to the inside to keep them out of the storm."

Feeling my urgency, Alba reined Bonita south, as she said, "We better get to hoofing it Mr. Mateo!"

Ripley had already figured out what the plan was and took point in front of Bonita. With one last look over my right shoulder towards the fast-approaching storm, I could see the lightning and hear the thunder. Reining Ella hard southward, I gave the mare some spur and 7 strides later I was neck and neck with Alba and Bonita.

The shit storm behind was gaining on us and sounded like a freight train bearing down on us. The wind had just in the last minute or two increased 10-fold, to the point it was pushing us faster than the horses could actually run. With another look over my shoulder, all I could see was a rolling gray and black cloud all the way to the ground filled with dust, pounding rain, lightning, thunder, and debris from buildings that had been in the storm's wake. Storm, hell, it was a full-fledge tornado that was bearing down on us. I feared that Ella or Bonita might stumble, because of the twister like winds. If they did and Alba or I got tossed from our horses, I doubt we would survive this storm in the open.

Alba and I were pushing the horses hard, and Ripley, Ella, and Bonita felt the urgency that was justified, given our circumstances. Ripley was in a full out run staying side by side with the horses. This run to Walmart and possible safety it could afford us had turned this ride into a do or die situation.

With no time to survey the exterior of Walmart, we finally turned the corner at a full gallop, and reached the back of the old abandon store. There were several long forgotten semi-trucks with their trailers still parked at the loading docks. There was a slanted ramp at the south end of the loading dock for those that used handcarts and forklifts. Ripley busted up the ramp, then Alba, still on Bonita, followed quickly. Just as I moved Ella into the position to go up the ramp, a 6 x 8 piece of galvanized corrugated piece of metal sheeting that had been launched and now swirling in the tornado almost took Ella and me out. How it missed us by just a couple of inches, I will never know, as Ella scrambled up the ramp.

Dismounting swiftly, I moved towards the man-door next to the garage door. The door was being slammed open and closed in the wind, since someone had kicked it in and compromised the door many years ago. Pulling my pistol and then crouching into a shooter's stance, I opened the door and ventured into the dark interior of the Walmart. If not for the small amount of light from the open man-door, the interior would have been pitch black. Locating the pull chain for the garage door, I started pulling downwards, and the old door needed oiling, but still worked. In a few seconds, I had the door opened high enough to admit access into the loading dock. Alba had both Ella and Bonita's reins in her hands, and she moved inside, leading the horses, then Ripley followed. Once everyone was inside, I quickly, still using the pull chain, lowered the garage type door.

Just as soon as the bottom of the garage door hit the concrete floor, sealing us off from the raging storm outside, Ripley, staring into the interior of the loading dock, growled. Then a man's voice spoke from the darkness, and said, "Greetings, Walmart shoppers!"

Obviously, we were not alone. And I knew he had the drop on us and was pointing some weapon at our backs. Ripley was on edge and still growling, without turning, I spoke in a calm voice,

"Mister, we are just getting out of the storm. We will be on our way as soon as it is done."

The man, in an unhurried voice, spoke again, "Try to settle your dog down, mister. I would hate to shoot that splendid-looking canine, but if it attacks, I will kill it!"

Now, why did he have to threaten my dog? Nothing makes me madder than when someone threatens my dog! Still without turning, "Just know Mister, if you shoot my dog, that will displease me very much, and you don't want to see me displeased!"

But since, at this very moment, I was not in any position to argue, I said, "Ripley, quiet down, and sit." Ripley was not happy about that command, but did as I had asked, and she quit growling and then planted her butt onto the concrete floor.

The loading dock garage doors were shaking violently and rattling with each gust of wind. The entire building was moaning and groaning as the steel structure was flexing into the fury of the storm outside. I was wondering if this Walmart was going to survive this storm.

The voice behind seemed to not have a care in the world, when the man chuckled, then spoke again, "Ripley? Don't tell me, you named your dog after Sigourney Weaver in those old Alien movies. Those movies have to be at least 60 years old. Is that where you got the name?"

"It is, and believe it or not, my dog before this one was named Bishop, after the android, from the 2nd movie in the series, the one called Aliens."

A light was turned on spotlighting Alba and I, then the voice behind us said, "Well, Mr. Movie Buff, both of you need to drop those holsters on the ground. And I mean slowly."

With a sideways look at Alba, I nodded my head in an affirmative. With a heavy sigh from both of us, we did as the man asked and released our holsters and let them slide slowly to the ground. Once that was done, without turning around, I spoke to the man behind us, "We have complied. Just let us ride out the storm here, and we will leave promptly."

The noise in the loading dock was loud, as the metal doors continued to flex in and out as the storm savaged the outside. The man behind us said, "The storm is a doozy for sure. Now I need you to pull out those knives and drop them on the floor next to your pistols."

Once again, Alba and I had no choice but to comply, as we dropped our knives at our feet. "Mister, we did as you asked. Now I am getting a little perturbed standing here next to this damn door that is about to be torn off from the freakin' tornado outside."

"Archer. Archer Bowman is my name. Now you the little one, you need to move closer to the taller one, so I can get a better look at both of you. I was able to find a case of batteries to fit my flashlight here, but the lighting in here still sucks."

Alba did as she was told. She dropped the reins of Ella and Bonita, and then moved closer to me. Apparently, Archer Bowman had failed to realize so far in the low light Alba was a woman. Not sure if that was a good thing or a bad thing. Once Archer was satisfied with our actions so far, he said, "Okay, Mr. Movie Trivia, what was the actor's name that played android Bishop in Aliens?"

Alba looked at me and raised her eyebrows. I did likewise, before I answered, "Lance Henriksen was his name. His character Bishop was the science officer of the Sulaco. Ripley at first didn't trust him after what the android named Ash in the first film Alien had done. But, in the 2nd installment, Bishop would be critical to the survival of Ellen Ripley."

"Bravo, bravo, you are correct. I am proud of you. You know your 'Alien' movies! Now, listen carefully. I want both of you to turn around slowly."

Alba and I, as instructed, turned around slowly and faced the man that had been behind us. The man was dressed as a survivor and not as a Gunner or a Holy Joe. He was older than me by at least 30 years. Long gray hair with a long gray beard. He was wearing blue jeans, combat boots, and a hooded sweatshirt that had the former pro basketball team, the Denver Nuggets, stenciled across the front. What made the man dangerous, of course, was he was pointing at us an Enhanced Battle Rifle EBR, the exact same rifle I had riding in the scabbard on Ella. By the way Archer Bowman held the rifle, I had zero doubt he knew how to use it. At this moment, Mr. Bowman had Alba and me at his mercy.

As soon as Alba and I had finally turned to face the gunman, and the light of his flashlight showed who we were, he chuckled, and said, "Whoa, I will be damned, look at that, the little one is a woman. And a good-looking one at that!"

Alba's face snarled up as she said, "You touch me. I will cut your heart out!"

"And a feisty one at that. I respect that tone, young lady. And hopefully this will ease your mind. The one and only love of my life died back in 2021 of the Delta Variant. In my heart, she is still there, in my mind. I can still see her beautiful face, and I am still true to her. I have not longed for another woman since she died. You have nothing to fear from me."

That reply was not what I expected, and by the look on Alba's face, it was not what she expected as well. As we stood there, still dumbfounded by the gunman's heartfelt statement, he spoke again. "Well, you both know my name. What is yours?"

Although Mr. Bowman was still pointing his EBR at us, I was getting the feeling that he was a good man. And as long as we did not attack or threaten him, he would not shoot us. I smiled as I said, "My name is Dixon Mateo. And the feisty one is Alba Jesse."

Archer Bowman smiled, then he said, "Mr. Mateo and Miss Jesse, it is nice to meet you both. Are you hungry?"

Another statement that took me by surprise, when I said, "Ahhh, what?"

"I asked, are you hungry? I found a crate of lemon sparkling water and another one of Libby's Vienna Sausage in Chicken Broth."

It was Alba's turn to act surprised when she said, "Ahhh, what?"

"You know them little, tiny salty sausages packed into a small can. I already done eaten 2 cans before you showed up here. Oh hell, you might be too young to remember. Then you best just follow me." Having said that, Archer Bowman lowered his rifle and swung it over his shoulder and walked through the swinging doors to his right into the interior of the store.

Alba looked at me and raised her palms in confusion, and said quietly, "What the hell?"

I was even more confused than Alba. I shouted out after Archer, and said, "What about our weapons?"

Archer bounced back through the swinging doors with his rifle still riding on the back of his shoulder and pointed the flashlight at our weapons piled on the floor. "There is better light on this side of the doors from the windows and such. And I apologize, that was rude of me, here let me give you some light so you can gather up your pistols and knives."

As we almost in slow motion picked up our discarded weapons, in a very confused voice, I said, "Aren't you afraid we will use these on you?"

Archer Bowman laughed out loud this time. "The way I see it, any man or woman that name their dog after Sigourney Weaver is no threat to me."

Alba raised her palms again in confusion and said to Archer, "Have you actually ever seen the movie?"

CHAPTER 11

Ella and Bonita were too large to take through to the other side of the store. We tied them both off to some guard rails in the docking area. Both horses decide it was the time to drop a healthy shit right there on the concrete floor. Ripley slanted her head sideways as if she was contemplating doing the same thing. Alba looked at me with wide eyes, and then said, "Clean up on aisle 14!"

Given the circumstances, I busted out laughing. I would venture to guess in the history of Walmart that this was the first time that a horse took a crap in one of their stores. Alba and I both sort of shook our heads in disbelief.

After a good chuckle, Alba, Ripley, and I went through the same swinging doors that Archer Bowman had used to gain access into the front of the old abandon Walmart. You could feel the winds of the storm buffering against the north and west walls of the building, and you could see the walls move in and out with each gust of wind that slammed into the building. When looking through what was left of the front windows, it looked nasty outside. Debris was swirling and slamming into the building. I once again wondered if the building would withstand the storm or collapse because of it.

Archer Bowman had set up a small campfire the furthest away from the broken windows and the gusting winds of the tempest. He had pulled up a couple of couches that, at one time before the store had been abandoned, had been brand new. Now they were covered in the dust of what used to be. Alba and I took the couch opposite of Archer on the other side of the campfire. After wiping it off to rid it of the grime as best we could, we both then sat down. Actually, it was very comfortable for a decade old couch. As soon as we got our butts planted on the couch, Archer tossed us each a can of Libby's Vienna sausage in chicken broth, then said, "As promised, the little salty sausages!"

Alba held her can up for me to see, like it was some sort of prized possession. She then used the flip tab and pulled off the lid of the vacuum packed can. Alba then smelled the contents, when Archer said, "Try one, they are superb!"

Alba pulled her knife and cautiously stabbed one sausage and extracted it from the can. She smelled it once again and, with hesitation, stuck it in her mouth. I was watching, as I was content with letting Alba be the taste dummy on 40-year-old canned sausage. After swallowing, Alba smiled, and said, "These are delicious."

I quickly followed suit and opened my can and extracted one with my knife. After it went down, I said, "Hell, these are good!"

Once Alba and I completed eating our cans of the tiny sausages, Archer tossed us another can. It did not take long for Alba and me to eat 4 cans each, and Ripley ate 3 cans. In no time at all, we had our bellies full.

Archer had used old wooden pallets that he had broken up for fuel for the fire. Reaching out my hands towards the fire, it felt primitive, much like the days our ancestors sat around in caves trying to keep warm. I had gotten spoiled living in the Station with heat from the boilers. I had not had to resort to using campfires for cooking and warmth- yet. The fire reminded me, of the days before COVID and Tartarus when my mom and dad would take us up into Rocky Mountain National Park to go camping. The fire felt like those days with wonderful memories, and it felt good. There was enough light from the windows and the campfire that we could get a good look at the old man that sat across from us. Ripley ventured close to Bowman. Close enough that Archer reached out and gave Ripley a good petting. It would seem that by letting Archer pet her, Ripley had given her approval of the old man. Archer, after petting Ripley for a minute, went back to tending to the fire. To get the most warmth out of the flames, he was moving the slates of the shortened wood pallets into a teepee of sorts to get the best airflow through the wood. Obviously, he was very adept at doing such things. Every once in a while, his eyes would drift towards Alba and I. He showed no signs of being threatened by the 2 of us. Although I was leery of the old man, his actions showed no signs of being a threat to Alba or myself. Ripley now laid down in front of Archer. It would seem Ripley did not sense any threat from the man that just minutes ago had been pointing a rifle at us.

Archer Bowman was the oldest man I had seen in the last 20 years. Most of those of his age had died from the virus way back when Tartarus took hold and almost killed off all of humanity. Only the youngest and the healthiest survived those dark days. He seemed ancient in this world we now know. His face was wrinkled with time, which seemed fitting, given his grey hair and beard. Alba, just as I had been, was studying the man we were sharing a campfire with and she finally said, "Mr. Bowman, I am curious how a man of your age had survived the virus? I can't believe I have seen someone so old in the last couple of decades."

Archer Bowman laughed a hardy laugh, then he looked at Alba and said, "Man of your age? I think you mean an old fart such as myself! It is easy, Miss Jesse. According to those military quacks down in Cheyenne Mountain, I am the cure of all that ails us. I am some sort of genetic mutant. They didn't say exactly that I was a mutant, but that is how those bastards treated me and my brothers. Those nut jobs threw us in cells, poked, prodded, and studied us. They drew our blood as fast as we could reproduce it, and they injected shit into us to make us sick. The 3 of us were nothing more than guinea pigs to those government assholes. Both my brothers died at their hands before I escaped."

Alba looked at me, confused, after hearing Archer Bowman state he was the "cure." After seeing the same confused look on my face, she then glanced back to Mr. Bowman, then said, "I guess I am not following. They cured you of the virus?"

Archer popped the top on a can of sparkling water and drank the whole 12-ounce can of lemon flavor in one swig. After finishing, he crushed the can and smiled when he replied to Alba. "Not cured Miss Jesse, never had it. My 2 brothers and I never got vaccinated or any of the zillion boosters that came afterwards. We never even had a slight cough or runny nose. No respiratory illness ever. Everyone we knew caught one form of the different variants as the virus mutated down through the years. In the early years, as you know, there were deaths between 1 and 3 percent of the population, but most survived. The scientist of the earth thought the world was approaching herd immunity. Each time it tapered off; the virus mutated again. Then, around the 10-year mark after COVID escaped the labs in China, each new variant became deadlier until Tartarus. Tartarus proved to be the one that almost wiped out all the human species. By some accounts, it wiped out the remaining 95% of humanity, knocking humankind back into the Stone Age. Miss Jesse, have you or Mr. Dixon ever had the virus yourselves?"

Jesse looked at me, and previously we had talked about this very subject with each other. She knew my history, and I knew hers. Jesse turned back to Archer. "To answer your question, yes, both Dixon and I have tested positive for several of the variants over the course of time. In the early years, we took the vaccines that were offered, and the booster shots as needed. We both just assumed we had built up some sort of immunity to the virus as it mutated into different variants. Without knowing for sure, we just assumed we had been the lucky ones to this point and reached herd immunity that the scientists were trying to achieve way back when COVID first flooded the Earth."

The storm outside was not as intense, since the walls were not flexing in and out as they had been when the storm first hit. The creak and moan of the metal and concrete building had almost ceased. It would seem that the storm was tapering off and the building with us inside of it would survive another day. Archer tossed some more broken wooden pallets on the fire, then said, "It would seem this old Walmart has withstood the worse of the storm."

The old man intrigued Jesse and me. After he got the flame of the campfire to his liking, Archer spoke again, "Then you and Dixon have probably achieved what the scientists all along were trying to accomplish by saving the human species. It all seems sort of ironic to me it was the scientists that had unleased this hell on earth. And it was the scientists that tried to save humans from dying out. I guess they achieved success in that Dixon, and you are sitting here talking to me about this. After the fall of modern civilization, it plunged the world as we knew it into a dark period, which we are still in. What was left of man created kingdoms, clans, cults, and dictatorships across the world. It was and is a scary time. My brothers and I joined a clan, more for the protection it provided, than for any type of ideology. During one of the virus war battles, my brothers and I were captured by what was left of the American military. These blokes had taken up refuge in the Cheyenne Mountain complex that used to be the headquarters for NATO command near Colorado Springs."

I blurted out, "Yes, the Gunners!"

Archer smiled and said, "What?"

Clearing my throat, and replied, "My term for them is - Gunners. It is a name I made up to call those fellows from Cheyenne Mountain. They still make patrols even this far north. The only ones I know that still use helicopters and diesel- and gas-powered vehicles. I know they have taken some survivors prisoner. Those taken have never returned."

Archer smiled, then said, "Gunners! I like it, seems fitting. Before being captured but the 'Gunners', in all those years, my brothers and I never caught the virus or any of the variants. Never thought much about why, just thought we were lucky. We buried family and friends; those were sad days. We almost died in the riots and the virus wars that followed the fall and the destruction of the world governments.

After the Gunners captured me and my brothers, we were locked up with many other prisoners, with zero protection from Tartarus. No distancing, no masks, and no medications of any kind. Everyone in our cell block caught the virus and died. The only ones left were my brothers and me. It was then that the researchers working there in Cheyenne Mountain knew we were different somehow. They moved us into the research facility of the complex to study us.

The men in white lab coats separated us and put us in different cells. It is during this captivity that we became lab rats. The researchers poked and prodded us. They drew blood 3 times a day, trying to see why we were different. The researchers seemed to be amazed that we not only never got sick from Tartarus, but we had none, zero, and nada, antibodies of the COVID variants, that had come and went over the years. They injected us with all the different variants of COVID, including Tartarus. Once the scientists realized for whatever reason my brothers and I, not only never had the different variants, but that we would never get them. The Bowman brothers baffled them. Not once did we ever get sick, and they could not understand why. It was at this point that they injected other diseases such as malaria, HIV, and even Ebola, to see if any germ or disease had any effect on us. Nothing made us sick, nothing those relentless bastards did to us would faze our bodies' immune system. Looking back in retrospect, I realized that none of us had actually ever been sick in our lives, not even any cold or flu.

My oldest brother Gary's theory was that God ordained and blessed us. That we were the ones that would inherit the earth. My younger brother Bruce believed we were immortal. The isolation that we were in, and the constant back and forth between the labs and our jail cell, played havoc with our minds. Our bodies remained healthy, but our minds lost touch with reality. We started slowly to go stir crazy in those dark and lonely cells in Cheyenne Mountain. Not sure about my brothers, but the thoughts of taking my own life flowed freely through my mind. I never had the courage to actually do it, but the thoughts plagued my dreams when I slept.

In time, the older scientist actually succumbed to the Tartarus virus they were studying and died. The younger and healthier ones lacked knowledge and guidance in their studies on us, they lost their focus, and in some ways, I think they forgot why or how my brothers even came to be there in their research facility. In some ways, I think the younger scientists feared us. To my knowledge, I do not believe the researchers ever came to a scientific understanding of why the Bowman brothers were how we were. In time, with no actual answers, what was left of the research team lost interest in the Bowman brother's altogether. We became more of a hindrance than the biological wonder and cure to Tartarus when we were first sent to the research center.

The remaining scientists just left us in our cells all alone. They fed us, but the food rations over time became less and less. It was my belief the facilities stored food was running low, and with as many mouths to feed in Cheyenne Mountain, it was the prisoners that went without. My brothers and I were malnourished, and we were dropping weight fast. Just like the photos I had seen of the German extermination camps in World War II. I had resigned myself that our fate was to die in those cells.

I had lost track of time during my brothers and my captivity, since we were never let outside of the underground bunkers of Cheyenne Mountain. We never saw the sun or the moon. Without clocks, sunrises, and sunsets, we had no way to track time. My estimation it was the 8th or 9th month when the power failed at the facility and the electronic locks on our jail cells clicked and the metal doors slowly swung open.

At first, I thought it was some sort of trap. No one came to check on us when the emergency lights kicked on. We were so hungry we raided the small refrigerator the researchers kept in their break room. The only food in that fridge was a jar of pickles and a dozen eggs. We ate the eggs raw, and the pickles only lasted a few seconds before we finished them. With a little food in our bellies, we worked our way up through the stairwells to the ground level floor. Soldiers rushed about, trying to restore power to the facility. There was a lot of yelling and rushed activity."

The tornado and the storm's wind became eerily silent. It was as if death had walked into this old abandon store as silence flowed over us. Archer stopped his telling of his tale and we all looked about, stunned by the sudden difference in the atmosphere of this old Walmart. The air temperature had risen quickly, and then dropped just as fast as a rolling crescendo of ear-shattering thunder reverberated across the roof and through the walls of the store. Then a blinding lightning flash followed directly after the thunder, then the hail started thumping the roof and the north walls. Not small hail, but huge roof piercing hail.

CHAPTER 12

The first baseball hailstones that punched a hole in the roof slammed into the concrete floor not 10 feet away from Alba, Archer, and me. The hailstones were so hardened by the fall from the heavens that they didn't even shatter after crashing into the floor, they just bounced. If we got hit by one, we would be severely injured. I didn't even want to think about what would happen if one hit us in the head.

Ripley was barking frantically and when Alba and I cuddled together to make a smaller target, Ripley laid on top of us, protecting us. After the initial onslaught, and we had gathered our collective wits. Archer pointed at a shelf behind us, seeing what he was pointing at, all three of us as fast as we could, pulled down an old musty, and gritty mattress and pulled it over us as we laid on the floor. Alba had pulled Ripley under the mattress and held her tight to her chest. No sooner than we had gotten settled under the mattress, that 2 hailstones hit the mattress with such force that if it had not been for the protective layer, the hail surely would have killed one, possibly 2 of us. If we survived this hailstorm, the 1st thing I was going to do was write a 10-star review for Tempur-Pedic, the manufacture of the mattress.

The storm and hail tapered off almost as fast as the storm began. Once we thought we were safe, we pushed the grungy old mattress off and stood up, eyeing the damage to the roof. There were hundreds of holes punched through. Archer said, "That's it, I am never shopping here again!"

Just as the thought crossed my mind, Alba voiced it, "The horses!"

We all ran through the doors onto the loading dock to see how Ella and Bonita fared during the storm. The hail had caused considerable damage to the roof of the loading dock area. Unknowingly, at the time Alba and I had tied the horses off under a solid metal mezzanine, we did not know that it would provide another layer of protection for the horses from the hailstorm. We were lucky—this time. Ella, Bonita, and Ripley were feeling happy to see each other, and the horses were using their noses to nudge Ripley playfully.

Seeing how we were all safe and unharmed, I said to Alba, "I wonder how bad the Station got hit?"

Alba's face mirrored my concern and said, "Looks as if we have overstayed our welcome here at Walmart. We might as well head home and see the damage there."

Archer had overheard our conversation, and then asked, "Station? What is the Station?"

Alba gave me that puppy dog look and grabbed my arm, and we walked far enough away that Archer Bowman couldn't hear us. Then she said, "What do we do about Mr. Bowman?"

"He was fine before he met us. He will be fine after we leave him be."

Alba's face turned a tad dark, then said, "Dixon, he has no one but himself. He is old. He could have killed us and robbed us of Ella, Bonita, weapons, and our other things, but he didn't. Instead, he offered us supper. He is a good and decent man. We just can't leave him here."

I had lived for so long by myself, hiding the fact that I had everything in the way of food, water, and electricity. I was hesitant to bring another person into the fold. As I was weighing the pros and cons of having another person live at the Station, Alba kind of huffed at my hesitance and said, "If we don't take him back to the Station, I am staying here with Archer, until you come to your senses! Plus, he didn't get to finish his story. We do not know how the immortal Bowman brothers died."

Made me chuckle. Alba was so intent on saving the last remaining Bowman brother; God I loved this woman. Smiling, I said, "Okay, okay, we will ask him if he wants to go home with us. You know, he might enjoy being alone. Some folks prefer it."

Alba's face lit up. She was happy, and said, "If he says he doesn't want to go, at least we asked him."

Alba grabbed my hand, and we walked back to Archer, when I said, "The Station is where we live. We have plenty of food, water, and electricity. You can even take a long, hot shower."

Archer Bowman thought about what I had said, then he said, "I am not looking for handouts. I may look it, but I am not a charity case."

Alba said, "That thought never crossed our minds, Mr. Bowman. You will earn your keep at the Station, there is a lot to do and maintain. You will be free to leave at any time if you think that is what you want to do. In truth, you would be helping us."

Archer thought some more, he smiled, then said, "I am sort of tired of wandering from place to place. And I am homeless. But I am not taking a hot shower with sonny boy here to conserve water."

We all had a good-hearted laugh at that. It felt good. It seems that we had taken in a rescue person and re-homed Archer Bowman.

The large hailstones that were scattered throughout the building were already starting to melt, leaving huge water puddles on the concrete floor.

Archer, Alba, and I worked like a well-oiled machine as we prepared Bonita and Ella to move out. It was like we all had been together for a long time. The feeling of belonging and friendship seemed natural to me. This feeling was refreshing and almost overwhelming when Archer had jumped in to help. Alba was beaming. I could feel her confidence and happiness in our decision to bring Archer into the fold. Archer seemed excited about the new arrangement as well. I was feeling better about having Archer join our clan. Clan? That word was never part of my vocabulary until Archer had brought it up earlier. But now it seemed fitting. My understanding of the word was that it meant - a group of people with a strong common interest. My definition made sense. We now were 3 people bonded together in a difficult time to survive this apocalyptic life we now found ourselves in.

Once we had the horses' saddles adjusted, the thoughts of what damage we might find at the Station flooded my thoughts. Having Archer in our midst would help in any repairs that may be required to keep the Station running as it had before. First things first, we had to get there and see exactly what we were up against.

I was so busy with the task of getting the horses ready and my thoughts of what was to come when we got to the Station; I had not been paying much attention to Ripley. Ripley had been at the closed loading dock door, as if she was using her canine attributes to sense what was beyond the door. I moved towards the chain pull on the door and Ripley moved in front of me and growled in a low tone to stop me. She had my attention now. Something or someone was beyond that door.

Raising my hand to silence Alba and Archer, I moved close to the door and pressed my ear against it. At first there was no sound other than the wind, until I heard a voice on the outside, "Jeremiah, tell me again exactly what you thought you heard?"

Obviously, there was over more than person just beyond the loading dock door, when I heard a reply, "I thought I heard a horse neighing. I was standing here, and it sounded as if it came from inside."

I slowly backed up, trying not to make a sound. Ripley backed up with me. Once I reached Ella, I pulled my EBR rifle from my scabbard and mouthed the words so Alba and Archer could see me "We got company".

With hand signals, I indicated we spread out, and for Alba and Archer to go into hiding. Archer went south, and Alba went north, as the man-door on the loading dock started to gradually open. I could see first a rifle barrel, then a man slowly emerged not over 30 feet away from Ripley and me. As he stepped inside, it took his eyes several seconds to adjust to the dimness of the interior of the Walmart loading dock.

Once his eyesight became accustomed to the low light, he saw Ripley and me standing next to Ella and Bonita. It startled him and he jumped. What he saw was me with my EBR pressed to my shoulder and pointed in his direction.

The man was wearing the white collar of the Cleric, or Holy Joes, as I called them. He belonged to the order that we had shot it out with at the feed store. Once the Holy Joe realized I had him at a disadvantage, he stood motionless as we stared at each other. I spoke first, "Greetings to Walmart. As you can see, we are closed today for some much-needed repairs."

The disciple of Joseph Spawn eyes squinted, not appreciating my humor at the moment. Before he could say anything, another man moved through the door and stood behind the first one, waiting for his eyes to adjust to the shadowy light of the dock area. The 2nd man said, "Did you say something?" Once his eyes adjusted, he saw what the first man saw, and that was me standing there pointing a rifle in their direction.

Once the 2nd man realized I was there, he exclaimed, "Oh shit!"

The first man was the leader. I could tell by his demeanor, I moved closer so he could see me better. Ripley stayed in between us, ready to move in if given the command. I said, "How many?"

The man in front didn't even hesitate as he answered, "Just the 2 of us."

Alba stepped out of the shadows and showed herself, then said, "He lies. I peeked out of the furthest door. Including these 2, there are 7. All are heavily armed and riding horses. They are a raiding party and ready for war."

A band of Holy Joes, a bunch of religious zealots. They had us outgunned and out-manned, in a clear voice, "What are you doing here? What are you looking for with a war party?"

The leader's eyes narrowed before he spoke, then he said, "If you are the man, I think you are. We have been looking for you for a week now! Mister, we came hunting for you!"

CHAPTER 13

This guy had a pair. I was pointing an enhanced battle rifle at his chest with only 30 feet separating us and his reply sounded like a threat. Alba was off to his left with her 9 mm Beretta pointed at his head as well. Archer had not made an appearance yet, but if I had to guess, I would venture to say he was also pointing his weapon at these 2 gents. I should shoot this Holy Joe just for being cocky. Instead, I held my trigger finger and said, "Looking for me? Now why a follower of Joseph Spawn would be looking for me?"

The leader of this war party looked determined. He was about 6 feet tall with long scraggly brown hair tied into a ponytail. The one in charge was muscular and obviously fearless, or maybe he was just stupid. He didn't even blink twice, knowing I was pointing my rifle at the center of his chest, right where his heart was. Maybe this zealot of God didn't have a heart. The leader was still looking at me, but when he spoke, it was meant for the one standing behind him. "Jeremiah, is this the man that you saw at the feed store? The one that killed 3 of our flock?"

The one standing in back must have been the one that got away during the feed store battle. Jeremiah was smaller with long dirty blonde hair. He was scrawny, and weak looking, and not as fearless as his commander. He had high-tailed it away from the feed store as fast as his horse could carry him, not wanting any part of the fight that killed his 3 compadres. Jeremiah, the one standing behind, didn't look smarter, but he must have been. He seemed to know if I pulled the trigger of the EBR from this distance, the bullet would probably penetrate the man in front and take him out as well. Jeremiah stayed silent as he stood there sweating. He was nervous and scared. He didn't want to die today.

The leader of this regiment of God's soldiers was getting impatient. He spoke in a louder and more stern tone, "Jeremiah, is this the man or not!?"

Jeremiah didn't want to speak. He had already shown his true colors when he fled the battlefield at the feed store. The leader of this bunch of fanatics was now getting angry, and his goodwill towards one of his own, Jeremiah, had run its course. He no longer cared if Jeremiah would identify me. In his mind, I was the one he was looking for, and that I, and anyone with me, would pay the price for what happened at the feed store. The leader's eyes glazed over even more when he stared at me with hatred of who I was, in a heightened voice he spoke, "Just know, you and anyone that is with you, it is God's Will that you should be sanctified!" The leader started to bring his rifle up, showing his intent to kill me.

"You are one crazy son of a bitch! You should have known better than bringing the ole stink eye and giving me it, when I have the advantage in a gunfight!" As soon as those words crossed my lips, with my rifle already to my shoulder, I pulled the trigger of the EBR.

The sound of the bullet hitting flesh, then penetrating, then hitting flesh again, was 2 dull thuds so close together, they sounded almost as one. Both the leader and Jeremiah dropped their weapons as they crumbled to the floor, blocking the door.

They both were unmoving, showing they were dead to this world. One bullet had pierced and killed both of the Holy Joes.

Archer moved quickly to my side and said, "That was nice of them fellas to line up for you like they did, so you could save on ammo. Hate to break it to you sonny boy, but the other 5 Clerics have dismounted and now are working up their courage to storm the building. Have you ever heard of the military term - Shock and Awe? And if you have, do you understand what it means?"

Momentarily stunned and looking at the 2 men that I had just killed, Archer's question brought me back to reality. Thinking of what I knew about, Shock and Awe. Shock and Awe was technically known as rapid dominance. It is a military tactic based on the use of overwhelming fire power and spectacular displays of force to paralyze the enemy's perception of the battlefield and destroy their will to fight. I answered Archer's questions, "Yes, and yes!"

Archer quickly asked, "At this Station you call home, how are you set up for ammo?"

Spinning my forefinger in a circle to indicate all of us, meaning Alba, Archer, and myself, I said, "We have plenty. We are not short of ammo."

Archer nodded his head in understanding and then took over the tactics to defend ourselves against the remaining Holy Joes. Archer, in a commanding but hushed tone, said, "Alba, you take the north door again. I will take the south door. These fanatics are young, so they will have little or no actual military training, and will come to this center door, because that, so far, is where all the action has been. They think they are up against one, maybe 2 people. Having the advantage in numbers will not save them. They do not know about Ripley or me. That is our advantage. When they get to the door and before they enter, Dixon your job, is to fire every bit of ammo you have into the man door and the loading dock door. Do not wait for a target. Just keep firing. Keep them outside and on the exterior platform. They will try to scatter, keeping their heads down low. That is when Alba and I will open up on them and catch them in a crossfire. We are going to take the starch right out of them and those priest collars they wear. Believe me when I say 30 seconds of that. If any of them are still alive, they will want no part of us."

Archer pointed towards the north door, and Alba ran into position. Archer moved towards the south door. Ripley and I would hold this ground waiting for the Holy Joes to make good their assault on the building.

I had a line of fire to both the man door and the loading dock door. This trip to the neighborhood Walmart had not been boring. First a tornado, then the hailstorm from hell, and now a firefight with a bunch of religious nuts. Almost felt sorry for them as they approached the center door. This would not end well for them. They were trying to use stealth; they were inexperienced in that regard. I could hear them as they moved towards the center door, just as Archer predicted. Once I saw a shadow appear at the man door, I opened up with everything I had. Emptying half of the ammo in the EBR at the man door, I then finished it off firing knee high into the loading dock door as I imagined the Holy Joes ducking for cover as they tried to make good their escape. Once the enhanced battle rifle was empty, I palmed my Uberti pistol and continued to fire into the door until it was empty, as Archer instructed. The sound of all of us firing at once was deafening inside the interior of the loading dock. It seemed like the non-stop continuous firing took forever, but in 30 seconds, it was over. The smell of spent shells and hot brass filled the air. The Walmart battle had ended.

Using the pull chain to raise the door, to view the aftermath, I was sickened by what I saw. The door had barely cleared an inch when the blood of the Holy Joes flowed underneath. Once the doorway was up a couple of feet, I could see the bodies of 3 of our assailants as they laid unmoving on the platform. Once the door was fully up, Ripley and I moved towards the exterior, reloading my EBR and my pistol as I exited the interior. After stepping over the 3 bodies by the loading dock door, I saw the remaining 2. They lay dead on the ground next to the concrete platform. After being caught in the crossfire in between Alba and Archer, they had fallen over the guardrail and had died where the semi-trucks used to backup to unload their merchandise.

Alba and Archer joined me on the platform as we surveyed the hell that we had unleashed on those that had hunted me. This place, this time, was relentless. Tartarus had kicked the human species backed thousands of years, back to the Stone Age. We killed these men, these Holy Joes, to survive. There was no joy in what we did. I felt nothing, no remorse, no happiness. Taking the life of those that meant you harm, only meant you survived another day to face what this world we now lived in, had in store for you in the next hour, the next day. Death was all around us, trying to erase our bodies and our memories from this Earth. Sometimes I wondered if the struggle was worth it. Just as that thought cross my mind, Alba slid into my arms and snuggled up close. Looking at this woman that I had fallen in love with, I realized, hell yes, it was worth the struggle.

The carnage that lay before us sickened me. Taking the "Holy Joes" lives had been quick and easy, almost godlike in some ways. Some of those that we had slaughtered and ambushed were young enough they had never known about life before Tartarus. They had never known the simple joys of what used to be. Long drives in the country. Throwing a Frisbee to your dog. Pushing a pigtail girl in a swing, as you gathered the courage to kiss her for the very first time. They had been born and raised in these savage times and had died a savage death. This entire event had saddened me, and I longed for a simpler time. We had survived, and they had not. That was all I could say about the deaths of these men.

What worried me the most about myself was I had lost count of the lives that I had taken since Tartarus had ravaged the world. Death faces haunted me at night sometimes; I had just added more faces to that carnival of lost souls that was deep within myself-conscious. To survive, it had become my second nature to kill. The 5% that had survived Tartarus, along with me, had been changed in the aftermath of the deadliest virus that the world had ever seen. It was not pretty what humanity had become. Had we lost our soul? Did we ever have one? Tartarus had laid its claim to those that it had not killed. It had transformed us into something that was not civilized anymore.

Alba walked up next to me and grabbed my hand, looked me in the eye, and then said, "Dixon, I feel it too. I feel that sorrow, which you are feeling. It was these men or us. Unfortunately, they hunted you and this is what they got. We are alive. You, me, Ripley, and Archer. We survived for a reason; we most get past this! This Earth is scorched and in shambles right now. We cannot allow our lives to take on the identity of the carnage that lies smoldering all around us. Of the death that lies at our feet. Maybe the reason we survived so far, that it is our destiny and fate to create something that indisputably declares we are not what lies strewn at our feet. That we band together to create successes that declare we are not this! That we are better than these men. Dixon Mateo, I love you, and I would not love a wicked man. You are good, we are good together. Just remember that."

Ripley moved in and nudged my leg as if she was trying to comfort me as well. I pulled Alba in for a hug, and we held each other for what seemed a long time. I closed my eyes and tried to wish the bodies that laid at our feet - away. Opening my eyes, they were still there. Still embracing the woman, I loved, I whispered in her ear, "Yet, the carnage remains. Thank you for your words, my love. I will try to get past this and remember that it is our love that is priority. Our survival is the priority. Thank you for being you."

Breaking Alba's and my embrace, I looked past the bodies of the men we had killed. Most of their horses had bolted during the shootout, but 3 remained. They had calmed down and now were grazing the wild grass and weeds that had grown in the concrete medium at the back of the Walmart store. Without looking at

Archer, I spoke to him, "Archer, have you ever ridden a horse? Do you know how to ride?"

Archer responded, "Been awhile since I have been on horseback, but yes, I know how to ride."

"We can make room at the Station for another horse. Let's see if we can gather one up for you."

Leading Bonita and Ella out of the loading area of the store and down the sloped ramp of the loading dock, we tied them off as far away from the dead bodies of the Holy Joes as we could. We decided that Alba, who would seem less intimating, would approach the Holy Joe horses and try to gather up one of their reins.

Alba slowly walked towards the Holy Joe horses and spoke to them in a sing-song voice. All 3 horses took notice of Alba. Not only did they perk up to her voice, but they also moved towards her without caution, as if she was a horse whisperer. In a few seconds, the horses had all but surrounded Alba and presented her with their muzzles to be petted. Alba's face lit up and with the largest smile I had ever seen on her, she turned back to Archer and myself, then said, "Can we keep all 3?"

It was as if the horses sensed Alba was an angel here on Earth, and that she represented all the good that was left in this world. In this pleasant and surreal moment, I almost didn't want to be the voice of reason, but someone had to be. I said, "Alba, unfortunately no. We only have enough room and feed for 3 horses. We can only take one."

Alba frowned a little at that, then she looked back at Archer. "Come pick your horse out, Mr. Bowman."

Archer was standing next to me, and said, "You know that your woman is really something special."

"I know. Make her happy and go pick a horse."

Archer approached the horses and all 3 now moved in towards him as he spoke in a hushed tone to them. Took him all, but 30 seconds to decide he wanted the white, black, and tan Colorado Ranger mare. The mare was all of 16 hands and muscular. These horses look similar to solid-block Appaloosas. The difference is Colorado Rangers can trace their ancestry to two Turkish stallions (Patches and Max) in the Colorado High Plains. This breed has a gentle nature with a short back and sloping shoulders. I had ridden some years ago and the ones I rode had been fun to ride.

Archer's new horse was still saddled. Alba knew Bonita, that the Holy Joes had stenciled under the rear skirt of the saddle her horse's name. She raised the skirt of the newest horse, and the name Ladybird was stenciled there. Alba walked to the head of the horse and whispered, "Is your name Ladybird?" The ranger mare responded by nudging Alba with her nose. It would appear that the mare's name was indeed Ladybird. Without hesitation Archer moved in and with the grace of a much younger man, was able to step into the stirrup and get himself planted into the saddle. He held the reins like a seasoned rider and reached down and patted his horse on the neck, and then said, "Ladybird, let's take a spin through the neighborhood to get to know each other."

CHAPTER 14

Archer and Ladybird were gone about an hour, and I worried maybe Archer had been thrown from his horse. I was just about to voice my concern to Alba when Archer on Ladybird, in a full gallop, turned the corner of the building. Archer's smile was as big as all outdoors. Alba laughed out loud when she saw them, and said, "I think Mr. Bowman approves of Ladybird!"

Archer pulled the reins back, and Ladybird came to a complete halt in front of us. It would seem that Archer and Ladybird had been meant for each other. Dismounting his new horse, Archer's grin said everything, but he spoke, "Yes, by golly, Ladybird is a keeper."

Since it would seem that Ladybird was the one and only for Archer. Alba and I moved towards the other 2 Holy Joe horses and took their saddles off. They would be free to roam wherever they decided to go. They could find their way home back to the Joseph Spawn compound in Brighton or return to the wild. But they would do so without being encumbered by their saddles.

As Alba and I unsaddled the horses, Archer set about gathering up all the weapons of the dead Holy Joes. I saw him as he started this task and said, "We really don't need those weapons. We have plenty at the Station."

Archer stopped and turned towards me. "I figured as much. Dixon, it doesn't matter if we need these weapons. What matters is that we deprive the enemy of which you are at war with, the chance to recover them."

I thought about what Archer had said, then I replied, "I am not at war with Joseph Spawn or anyone, for that matter."

Archer then pointed at the dead Holy Joes that we had killed just over an hour ago, then said, "Make no mistake, those men laying there with our bullets in them were here to make war on you and yours. They died trying to do just that. Dixon Mateo, like it or not, you are in a war. Not one that you had chosen, but one that has been and will continue to be waged on you. I know you would rather just forget this entire event that happened here today. But mark my words, son, Joseph Spawn and his radicals are at war with you. Once these fellows do not return, Joseph will send another patrol with more men and more weapons. If they find these bodies or not, they will still blame you for what happened here. They now have lost men in 2 different battles in this neighborhood. The Holy Joes will know you are close. They will continue to look for you, or I should now say, our clan. They will not stop; they will not give up. Our Clan, you Dixon, will be everything that Joseph Spawn preaches against to those zealots that follow him. By killing these soldiers of his and those that you killed before at the feed store, you have become the ultimate enemy. You, Alba, Ripley, the horses, and me have become the sole purpose for their existence. My new friend, they will not stop until you and yours are dead. I learned something long ago that the quick road to defeat in any war is not being adequately prepared. Our newly formed clan doesn't want war. We want peace, but we should be prepared for war and to be strong and cunning as we can be."

Archer had voiced what I already knew. War with Joseph Spawn and the Holy Joes was not what I desired. The radical in Brighton desired it. These men we had killed today were a testament to that. Down through history, every war when it comes, or before it comes, is represented not as a war but as an act of self-defense against a bloodthirsty maniac. Archer was right. Like it or not, our clan was at war. Looking at the dead bodies of those we had killed today, I realized that only these men, in their death, had seen the end of this war with Joseph Spawn and the Holy Joes.

Looking at the older and obviously a much wiser and more experienced Archer Bowman, "You are right Mr. Bowman, I have much to learn from you. Destiny has thrown us together for a reason."

Archer nodded his head in understanding. "I am going to say it now, to get it out there, because it is the truth and you both need to hear this. War is the remedy that our enemies have chosen. Eventually, we will be forced into giving them all they want."

Once all of our horses were ready, we moved eastwards towards the Station. We left those that we had killed where they had fallen in battle. Leaving the bodies to rot in the Colorado sun was brutal and not the Christian thing to do, but my faith in God had been challenged more than once since Tartarus ravaged the land.

As we moved closer to the station, I noticed that the damage done to the trees and buildings was not as severe as what had been done to the old Walmart. The hail size had gotten considerably smaller as we moved east in the Station's direction. This was good news. Hopefully, our home received minimal damage or none.

Another half-hour Alba, Archer, Ripley, and the horses had made it to the west side of Quebec Street, and as always, we pulled up near the old bus ride shelter and bench. Taking my field glasses, I surveyed the abandon Commerce City Municipal and police station building across the open field in front of me for at least 30 minutes. I saw no movement of any kind. I saw nothing that would show the Station was not as we had left it.

Since it was the middle of September, the temperature was dropping. As the sun started to finish its day and tuck itself behind the mountains to the west, the night air began to roll in.

Archer looked across Quebec Street and the field and said, "If that is the building you are living in, it would be difficult to defend if they ever attacked us."

Alba and I both smiled, then Alba said, "Not all is as it seems to be, Mr. Bowman. We only have to defend a small portion of the building."

After Alba spoke, I also added, "Archer, Alba is correct, but once you see the setup we have, I am more than interested in your thoughts on how to make it even better than it is. I am open for suggestions."

Archer, although silent, didn't seem to be convinced that the Station was the best place for us as we rode the horses across the field to the east. I knew that would change once we got inside, and he saw the advantages that we had.

As we got closer to home, I realized that the hailstorm that had so devastated the Walmart had not traveled this far eastward. What was left of the summer grass of the field we were riding across was still standing up straight, with no sign of hail damage. That was the best news we could have had.

Each time I have had to repair the Station, be it the roof, HVAC equipment, electrical, plumbing, the windows were getting tougher each time. Spare parts and material were now almost nonexistent. There would come a time when repairs would not be workable. Hopefully, no more repairs would be needed for a while.

When we reached the garage door and used the electronic code to lift the door into now what was a barn with horse stalls, Archer seemed impressed.

We released Ladybird, Ella, and Bonita into the barn area. As soon as the horses were unsaddled, groomed, and fed a bit of grain, Archer and I also gave each a generous amount of hay pellets. There were only 2 stalls, but since we now had another horse to care for, Archer and I laid out the area for a new stall to build for his horse, Ladybird.

Alba and Ripley stood outside while Archer and I took care of the horses, and were watching the sunset, when Alba stepped back in, and said, "You both might want to come and see this."

There was no alarm in Alba's voice, so Archer and I took our time going out to see what she was talking about. When I got to Alba's side, she was facing west and there was a huge grin on her face. She then pointed. There were 5 horses keeping their distance from the Station but grazing on the remnants of the summer grass in the open field in front of our home. It would seem the horses of the Holy Joes we had killed at Walmart had followed us home. 3 of the horses still had their saddles on, and the 2 that did not were the ones that Alba and I had unsaddled there at the old abandon store.

Alba grabbed my hand, obviously pleased that the horses were in what served as our front yard. The night was just rolling in, and we had just put our horses away, so I said, "If they are still there in the morning, we will try to grab those with saddles and take them off."

Alba, still all smiles, rolled into my arms for a hug. "Sounds like a plan, Dixon."

Archer wasn't smiling as he watched the horses, then he said, "I hate to be the one that rains on this parade. Those horses being here are not a good thing. They are just like a road sign pointing to us."

Archer's statement confused me. "I don't think so. When they don't return home, Joseph Spawn's radicals will not know for sure in what direction to look for them."

Archer said, "Not so sure. There were 7 Holy Joes that we killed. I took one horse. That leaves 6 horses. There are 5 in this bunch. One of the Holy Joes' horses headed back home. Might mean nothing, it might mean everything. Got this sinking feeling that the horse that high-tailed it home is a bad omen."

That night we walked Archer through the complex and showed him everything, the guns, ammo, running water, hot showers, his own room, and the ample supply of foodstuffs. He was impressed, and he seemed to be a man that was not easily impressed.

While showing Archer the Station, I also explained my theory of hiding in plain sight, here in our home. After he rolled that around in his thinker for a spell, he actually agreed that probably was the best scenario. He thought aside from all of what we showed him that the Station could use some improvements in defending it, just in case hiding in plain sight was no longer possible. We spoke for a long time before bed, and his thoughts on how to improve the Station were great ideas and we decided in the coming weeks to implement some additional security measures.

The next morning, I checked the security cameras, and the 5 horses were still out front in the open field. After a quick breakfast, we saddled all 3 of our horses. We were going to round up the 3 Holy Joe horses that were still saddled and try to get them unsaddled.

The morning air was cooler than yesterday, and it reminded me of the upcoming winter with blowing snow, was not far off. Ever since Tartarus ruled the world, the weather on the planet had gotten more unpredictable. Not sure why that was, but back in the early 2000s there was a big push to get rid of fossil fuels because some believed it was speeding up climate change. Now that fossil fuels were almost non-existent, climate change was still ongoing. I, for one, don't know if fossil fuels sped up climate change or not, but the truth of the matter was that climate change was as natural as the sun waking up in the morning. That would explain why before human species walked the face of the Earth that this planet experienced at least 5 different Ice Ages. I was not sure how much longer we had before the first snowfall this year. Each year, it always seems to come a little earlier than the last.

Ripley was helpful in our little roundup, and it only took a few minutes to get the horses unsaddled. We kept these saddles as spares and as we were storing them away in our makeshift barn, the 5 Holy Joes horses went back to grazing. Alba was still all smiles watching the Station's horse herd. I joined her and watched the horses, then I said, "It would seem as long as that grass in that field holds out that we now have our own remuda."

Alba looked at me and raised her eyebrows, then asked, "Remuda? Never heard that term before."

Archer had joined us as we watched the horses, and he said, "A remuda is a herd of horses that ranch hands select their mounts from. The word is of Spanish derivation, for 'remount' meaning a change of horses. It was a term used back in the Old West. The person in charge of the remuda was known as the head wrangler. It would seem, Alba, you are now the head wrangler."

Alba thought for a minute, then said, "I like the idea of being the head wrangler."

After the Holy Joe horses were relieved of their saddles, we continued Archer's education of the Station. To show him around and introduce him to the different systems that went into maintaining our home. We spent time going over the plumbing, electrical, and HVAC systems. I explained to him how we still received flowing water from the South Adams County pumping stations. We finished out the afternoon by doing some light repair on the roof over the Station, getting it ready for old man winter.

At sunset, we were all a little tired and sat down to eat some supper. Once we had our bellies full, I couldn't contain my curiosity anymore. I looked at Archer, and then said, "Archer, you are one of the most interesting men that I have ever met. And the story you told when we first met you at the old Walmart has intrigued me to no end. Alba and I would like to ask you to finish your tale of how you escaped your captivity at Cheyenne Mountain. And of course, if you don't mind, we would also like to hear what happened to your 2 brothers."

CHAPTER 15

Archer's mood became solemn as he folded his arms and set them on the break room table, and he spoke. "As I had mentioned before, it was not until my brothers Gary, Bruce, and I had been taken prisoner and incarcerated at the Cheyenne Mountain complex near Colorado Springs that I realized that there was something different about us. I had never thought about it until that time. Becoming lab rats for the men in white coats made me see we were different. We all had sustained injuries and wounds down through the years, but none of the Bowman brothers had ever gotten sick."

Archer cleared his voice and continued, "The military scientists of Cheyenne Mountain didn't care about us as human beings; all they cared about was that we were test subjects. Have you have ever read ancient history about the Germans of World War II? About the Jewish concentration camps and the medical experiments that were conducted there as they carried the mass genocide out. That is how they treated us. We were freaks of nature, not people. We were simply guinea pigs. They did not know why my brothers and I were immune to not only the different COVID variants, but especially to the deadliest variant Tartarus.

While in custody of the Gunners scientist, my brothers and I self-awareness, was unraveling. Our sanity during that time was questionable. In short, the poking, prodding, and the isolation were slowly driving us insane. Gary, the oldest, thought God had ordained us. That the Bowman's and anyone else so ordained by God would inherit the earth. Bruce, the youngest, believed we were immortal. Personally, I became depressed. The isolation, the length of captivity, no sun, no fresh air, took its toll on me. My mind swirled around with thoughts of suicide."

Archer stopped for a few seconds, took a deep breath, and then continued, "What bothered me the most was the constant buzzing of the fluorescent lights. My cell, and my brother's cells, had them overhead, as did the hallways. Everywhere in those tunnels and labs had those lights. That buzzing and humming of the lights irritated me to no end. The forever buzz was and forever will be etched into my mind and subconscious. That 'buzz' drove me crazy."

Archer quickly nodded his head several times as if he was hearing the sound from the lights as he told his story. Another deep breath and he continued, "As time moved on, our food rations became less and less. All the experimentation, lack of sunshine, isolation, lack of food, and those damn fluorescent lights wore me down. When the older scientists died off from Tartarus, and with no actual answers on our immunity to the virus, the remaining younger and stronger scientists feared us. We were no longer the 'cure', but we became more of a hindrance. I suspected the food was running short at the complex, and it was the Bowman brothers that would suffer the most when the food ran out. My brothers and I were healthy men when captured, but in time, our physical bodies deteriorated. And it was my belief we would die of starvation in the cells under the mountain. You might ask how long were we prisoners of the Gunners? During the time in those cells, I couldn't answer that. Without knowing the passage of the days and nights, it could have been months, or maybe even years. I had no recollection of time. All I know was it seemed like time had stopped. After I escaped and could put together a timeline of our captivity at Cheyenne Mountain. Gary, Bruce, and I had been in those cells deep within the mountain for over 11 months. It seemed longer, a hell of a lot longer."

Archer was looking at the table and he tapped his fingers from his right hand loudly as he spoke again. "Something woke me up. I soon realized it was the silence. The constant buzzing from the fluorescent light bulbs suddenly stopped. It was eerie and surreal. The sound that was driving me crazy had ceased. I know it sounds irrational, but once the lights went out and in the total darkness deep within that mountain, I felt utterly alone without the sound of those lights. In some way, that buzzing had become my connection to the outside world. It scared the hell out of me, not the darkness. It was the lack of the buzzing sound. The darkness didn't last. It was only a matter of a few seconds and the generator, and the emergency lights kicked in. Not the fluorescent lights overhead, but the emergency lights on the walls that provided a gloomy light. There was no buzz from those lights, and at the time I was not sure I welcomed the silence. Since the cell locks were electronic, the cell doors popped open a few inches when the power went out, and before the emergency lights kicked on. I was in disbelief seeing the door open liked that. Thinking the open cell door was some sort of illusion. I got off my cot and walked to the door. Sure, as shit, it was open. My mind started racing with all kinds of thoughts. At first, I thought it was a trap, thinking they were trying to lure me out for some unknown reason. I stood there for several minutes trying to decide what to do, and then suddenly Gary and Bruce were standing there outside my cell. I had seen them both in passing in the hallways as the men in white coats had taken us into the different laboratories, but I had not seen my brother's up close in 11 months. They both looked weak, they both looked like death warmed over, and they both looked like shit. As did I."

Archer paused for a few seconds then spoke again. "Gary opened my cell door. Then he said, 'They are busy with the power failure. Let's get the hell out of here, while we can'. We were all starving and the first place we went was the scientists' break room. There was a little food; raw eggs and pickles, and we devoured all of that was there. We then went into the hallway and several soldiers rushed by us. They never stopped to question us. The ones we saw were in a panic of sorts. Losing electrical power had them scrambling. My brothers and I did not know where we were. No idea on how to escape or even if we could escape. We just started walking down one of the long hallways in one direction. After a few minutes, we came across a large sign on the wall. It was a fire exit sign. It showed us where we were in the complex and there was a dotted line towards the nearest exit. I tore the sign off the wall to use it as a road map, and then we just followed the dotted line. We were on the 3rd level below ground, and the elevators would not work on emergency power, so we had to use the stairways. We all were so weak we had to stop several times to rest and catch our breath as we climbed the stairs. Even though we had passed soldiers on the stairs, no one stopped us. It was as if we didn't exist. It took my brothers and me a long time to climb the stairs to get to ground level. Once there, we found a fire exit. We pushed on the crash bar and the door opened easily, with no alarm. Stepping outside, fresh air washed over us, and the sun was riding high in the sky above our heads. After being in the cold and clammy cells, the warmth of the sun felt good. It almost made me feel alive again. The biggest problem is that our eyes had become accustomed to the fluorescent light interior of the complex. The sunlight partially blinded us. Using my hand to shield my eyes, I could see not far away the entrance to the compound. Armed guards manned it, but the gate was open. Gary and Bruce started walking towards the gate. I followed. We had no plan, no thought, other than we needed to get away from that place. The guards finally noticed us making our way towards them when one yelled out, 'HALT!' We just kept walking as if we didn't hear him. As we continued, then they leveled their rifles and pointed them at us. Once again, the guard yelled, 'Halt or I will shoot you!' Gary was in the front, and he never even looked at or acknowledged the guard that was pointing his rifle at him. It was as if Gary's sole focus was on just getting out through that gate. Several seconds later, the guard pulled the trigger and shot Gary in the chest. Gary took one more step before his legs buckled and he fell hard onto the pavement. Bruce and I ambled to his side, and we both sat down next to our brother as he was dying right before our eyes. I had been in the military and saw battle in the Middle East. I had seen men shot before, and knew his wound was fatal. His weakened condition didn't help. It would not be long before he bled out. Gary, was looking at both of us as his eyes fluttered and his life was fading away, then he smiled, and said in an almost pleasant voice, 'Brothers, no sadness for me, I am going home!' His eyes fluttered once more, before he died."

This time Archer paused for several minutes as he regained his composure. Then his tale continued, "Because of our weakened condition, Bruce and I had to help each other stand. Slowly rotating my head in a half circle, I saw 6 guards now standing all around us with their rifles pointed in our direction. At that moment, I almost wished they had shot us both dead to end the misery. Just like Gary - Bruce and I were broken men. Our will to live had been tested and had languished in those fluorescent lit cells. The look on the guard's faces was that of sorrow and sadness. They, to a man, finally realized the condition we were in. They saw we were no threat to them, Cheyenne Mountain, or anybody, for that matter. I had the feeling those 6 men would have rather been some place other than confronting us. We all stood there for almost a full minute, when a voice behind said, 'For pity sakes, lower those rifles and let these men go. They have been through enough!' The soldier the voice belongs to stepped up and handed me a small backpack and 2 canteens of water. He said, 'There are a few survival items and 3 days' worth of freeze-dried food in there. It is the best I can do. We are all on starvation rations here, and you need to leave now, before my Captain sees that I have given you some food.' Bruce and I walked past the gate and left the complex of Cheyenne Mountain behind. Bruce was not as immortal as he once thought. He died in his sleep, 2 days after they had shot Gary. Both my brothers died 8 years ago."

As Archer told Alba and me the story of the death of the Bowman brothers, he never looked at us. He just stared at the top of the table as he spoke. Once the tale was completed, he lifted his head, and we could see his eyes. They were red and misty. He had just relived the sorrow of his captivity and the death of both of his brothers. He suddenly stood up and his voice cracked with emotion as he said, "Now you know about the 3 Bowman brothers. Not a pretty tale, by any means. I think it is time to turn in for the night."

Just as Archer finished talking, the lights in the Station blinked several times. The lights were a warning I had set up. Something or someone outside the Station had tripped the security alarm!

CHAPTER 16

Alba looked around, confused, and said, "Dixon, what is going on?"

"Someone or something has tripped the perimeter alarm! They have to be really close to do so. Alba, grab your weapons and move towards the horses and try to keep them quiet if you can. Archer and I will check the security cameras and see what we are up against."

Alba moved silently and quickly towards the makeshift barn. Archer, Ripley, and I posted up in the security monitor room. What we saw was alarming, but not dangerous yet. It would seem that a patrol of Gunners had bivouac in the field to the west where the Holy Joe horses had taken up refuge. There were 3 Humvees, one helicopter, and, by my count, 12 men. The soldiers were milling around a very large campfire, talking and laughing. Those that we could see were too far away to trip the alarm, meaning someone was or had been closer to the building.

Switching through the different cameras slowly, until finally one camera picked up those that had tripped the alarm. There were 2 soldiers, and they were walking casually around the building.

That made a total of 14 armed Gunners. The 2 closest to the building, rifles were slung on their backs, they seemed to be out for a stroll, nothing more. One seemed to be telling the other a story of sorts and was using his hands in animated gestures. These 2 soldiers did not seem to be looking for any entry points into the building, just walking on the north side of the building. Archer and I both knew these soldiers were far enough away from the horses to hear them, but that may change. We had to be ready in case they heard the horses and decide to investigate. Archer left the room and within a minute had returned. He had armed himself with the EBR rifle and a machete. Once I saw how he was armed, Archer said in a quiet voice, "If those 2 hear the horses or even seem to take an interest in where we keep them, I will try to take them out quietly."

I nodded my head in understanding. I was not sure how a machete could take out 2 men quietly, but in the short time I had known Archer Bowman, the one thing I have learned, was not to underestimate him. If he thought he could take them out quietly, I believed if any man could do it, that it would be Archer.

The 2 soldiers got to the northwest corner and looked to be turning in the direction that would take them right by the garage we had turned into a horse barn. This was not good news. Archer and I were relieved to see the soldiers had stopped and were facing due west, as if one of the other Gunners had caught their attention. The 2 strolling soldiers' complete attention was now focused on the Gunners' encampment. It would seem they were being called back to the campsite. The 2 that had been strolling around the building picked up their pace and headed directly towards the Gunners' camp and their huge campfire.

Looking towards Archer, I said, "I wonder how long they plan on camping in our front yard? It is obvious they do not know we are here, and they were not looking for us. I am also curious if it was just a remote chance encounter, they camped here. Archer, what do you think?"

"I do not think it was a coincidence. I have my suspicions. Can you locate and isolate the Holy Joe horses on your cameras?"

It took me several more minutes of switching back and forth until I finally could locate and see the Holy Joe horses. Archer was standing over my back as I focused in on the horses. Archer said, "Just as I thought."

I was looking at the same screen as Archer, and I was not comprehending what he was thinking. I finally turned in my seat and faced the older man. "Just as you thought, what exactly?"

"There were 5 horses, now we can only see 4 horses."

I ran that through my mind, and I was still coming up blank. "Still not seeing what you are seeing."

"They camped here in our front yard, not because it seemed to have a marvelous view. That big campfire is for the barbeque. They camped here, because there was fresh meat on the hoof. The Gunners butchered one horse for food."

During the next 3 days, we took shifts monitoring the Gunners. It almost seemed they had taken up permanent residence. In 8-hour shifts, one of us was always watching the security monitors. One of us always stayed with the horses. We assumed having someone caring for the horses the whole time would keep them as quiet as they could be. It was getting tiresome watching the Gunners from our vantage point. Archer, Alba, the horses, and I were getting Cabin fever. Ripley was getting stir-crazy inside and could not understand why we let her go to the bathroom in the barn area. She wanted and needed to be outside, just like all of us. We needed to feel the sunshine on our faces and breathe fresh air. We all wished the Gunners would just fade away.

On the 4th day towards sunset the Gunners started to slowly pack their stuff as if they were getting ready to pull out in the morning. Several hours past sunset, they were settling in for the night. They had posted 4 guards, keeping in with their normal routine. Ripley was sleeping at my feet, and I was having a hard time keeping my eyes open.

Around midnight, my eyes snapped open as the lights in the security room flashed on and off. The perimeter alarm had been tripped and someone was close to the building again. I was going slowly through the camera's angles, looking closely at what or who might have tripped the alarm. Alba was with the horses, and I had not set up to have the lights flash in the barn, thinking it might spook the horses. Alba would not be aware someone or something had a tripped alarm.

The flashing lights in the rest of the station had waken Archer, and he quickly joined me in the security room. He said, "Dixon, what do we have?"

Keeping my eyes glued to the security monitors, I said, "Not sure yet. Still searching."

A few minutes later, I was able to locate those that tripped the alarm. There were 2 men on the north side of the building. One was holding the reins of their 2 horses behind and to the east of the other man. The furthest west man was squatted down low and had a pair of field binoculars and was looking towards the Gunner's camp. Archer squinted at the monitor. "Are those 2 fellows who I think they are?"

"If you are thinking they are a couple of Joseph Spawn's men, then yes, I believe what we have here are a couple of Holy Joes. Probably looking for the patrol we took out in the Walmart battle. If not for the Gunners stopping here and having a hankering for fresh meat. These Holy Joes probably would have collected their horses and moved on. Hate to admit it Archer, but you were right. Those Holy Joes horses were a bad omen. The whole time I lived here in the Station, only once years ago did any Holy Joes get close. Now in the space of a week, not only do we have Holy Joes just on the other side of our walls of our sanctuary, but we got a shitload of Gunners parked right out our front door."

Archer nodded his head in understanding, then he said, "Dixon, there is nothing we can do about it now. It is what it is. Our only saving grace right now is that neither of these factions knows we are here. Hopefully, it stays that way."

Archer and I watched the disciples of Joe Spawn for another 15 minutes. All the one to the west did was keep his field glasses on the Gunners as if he was taking mental notes of equipment and manpower. So far, the Gunners guards were unaware of the 2 horse men. I panned back to the monitor of the Holy Joes, and I almost jumped back. The one holding the horses was looking directly at the camera.

Archer bent and looked closer at the monitor. The Holy Joe was fixated and still looking at the camera and his mouth opened as if he gasped. Archer said it before I did, "That son of a bitch suspects the camera is live. How he knows, I do not know. The look on his face tells me he knows he is being watched!"

Joe Spawn's man was still looking at the camera when he crept forward and tapped his buddy on the shoulder. The other Holy Joe almost jumped at being tapped, then looked at his cohort. Once the man that had been observing the Gunner's took notice of his partner, the 2nd man pointed upwards towards the camera then leaned down and spoke into the 1st man's ear. The man that had been spying on the Gunners looked over his shoulder at the camera for a few seconds, then shrugged his shoulders. The one with the binoculars was not buying what the other one was saying. Archer and I watched the entire exchange, not sure on how to proceed at this point. Archer finally spoke, "The guy with the field glasses is not concerned. He doesn't seem to care, not one iota. I wonder what spooked the first guy."

There was absolutely nothing we could do but wait it out. Hopefully, the 2 Holy Joes would be more concerned about the Gunner patrol and forget the conversation they just had about the security camera.

With one last look, the Holy Joe that had been observing the Gunners stood. And pointed to the east. Both of Joseph Spawn's men took the reins of their horses and faded into the darkness to the east, walking their horses quietly. The Gunner patrol had never known they were there. My gut instinct was telling me the man that noticed the camera was bad news. The look on his face told me he absolutely believed they were being watched, no matter what his comrade thought.

Archer said, "I still have 4 hours of sack time before my watch. I am going back to sleep. Let me know if the situation changes."

Watching Archer Bowman walk away back to his sleeping quarters, he walked as if he was a troubled man. I could tell that he had been just as disturbed by the Holy Joe's reaction as I had been.

The next 4 hours passed slowly, without incident. My mind was conflicted with thoughts of the Holy Joe, knowing he was being observed. After the Holy Joes had taken their leave, I almost felt sick to my stomach. I could not shake the feeling of impending doom. It had been a long night for me as the sun was making its presence known and broke the horizon in the east.

The Gunner patrol was already up and about finishing their packing. Where they were headed after this I did not know, nor did I care, as long as it was far away from the Station, we called home. Focusing in on the security monitor, I tried to find the Holy Joe horses that had been grazing in the field previous to the Gunners bivouac. No matter how long I searched for them, there was no sign of them. It was my fear that none of them had survived. I did not fault the Gunners on how they had filled their bellies. It was a simple fact that everyone, including those that might be our enemies, had to eat. Alba was heartbroken at what had happened to the horses. In the short time they were here, Alba had learned to love those horses.

Alba joined me in the security room, since it was her turn to monitor the Gunners. Archer would rotate into the barn area to tend to the horses. It was my time for some much-needed shuteye.

After only 4 hours of sleep, my eyes snapped open. My heart was beating a drum, and I was soaked with sweat. The dream that I had was disturbing. The Station had been ransacked and everything that I took for granted living there had been destroyed or taken. My, our sanctuary, had been exposed to what remained of the world. It had become unsafe, like everything outside of its walls. Alba, in my dream, was missing. In the dream, I did not know if she was dead or alive. Just a dreadful feeling that she was gone. Archer was not in the dream, but the feeling of him being dead was not in the forefront, just that he was not in the dream. I did not know what it all meant. My frantic search through the ruins of the Station for those that I cared and loved was a painstaking failure. Alba and Archer were nowhere to be found. I felt so utterly alone in the world.

I sat up in bed and relived every aspect that I could recall of the dream once again. I was searching for clues in my memory. It felt so damn real. Was this dream a premonition of what was to come, or was it just simply a dream? My stomach hurt and my mind was filled with dread. Seeing flashes of the dream run through my mind again and again, my gut instinct was telling me it was a vision. A vision of the future. A vision of the end.

CHAPTER 17

For the next week, after both the Gunners and Holy Joes had left the territory surrounding the Station, our routines went full circle and became the norm again. Each of us had fallen back into the chores that we each did around the Station to help maintain and keep our home functional and safe. Although the chores were the same, something was different. Our attitudes had changed, and we all were on edge. I think all of us, Archer, Alba, and me, were just waiting for the other shoe to drop. We did not feel safe in our sanctuary we called home anymore. I could not stop thinking of the Holy Joe's expression when he thought the security camera was operational and watching him.

The weather cooled off even more, and between the 3 of us, we felt confident we had prepared for the onslaught of old man winter as best we could. No snow, yet, but had a feeling this winter was going to be a rough one. We had enough hay pellets and grain for the horses. Our food pantry was still full of freeze-dried food. The boilers and heating equipment had been serviced, and we had changed all the filters in the fresh air intakes and exhaust.

Each night, after Alba had fallen asleep, I had trouble sleeping. The dream I had of the Station being in shambles kept creeping back into my thoughts. I tried to tell myself it was just a dream, and it meant nothing other than it was a dream. My gut was telling me differently. I was not sure if there was a next step to take, or if

I was just being overly nervous for no reason. So far, I had not mentioned to either Archer or Alba anything about the dream. I did not want them to think I was losing it, but in retrospect, my thoughts were, I should at least talk to Archer about it. I trusted him and his experience. Tomorrow, I will tell him and see what he thinks. It would be good just to get it off of my chest for now.

Alba and I woke up at the same time. We lay in bed for a while, enjoying the physical comfort of each other. I loved her more than life itself and making love to her in the early morning hours was the most wondrous thing. We broke into a sweat as we pleased one another, and afterwards Alba got up and kissed me full on the lips, just before heading to the shower. I watched her walk away, and she wiggled her butt, knowing full well I was watching it. It made both of us laugh. Once she was out of sight, the worry of my dream crept in again. If I lost Alba, for whatever reason, I am not sure I could go on without her. She truly was my—everything. The only thing I had to live for in this world of Tartarus.

I quickly showered and got dressed. Archer and I were going to ride and hunt the area surrounding what used to be the Rocky Mountain Arsenal Wildlife Refuge. We all had a hankering for fresh meat, and the refuge was still home to plenty of mule deer and buffalo.

Archer saddled Ladybird, and I saddled Ella. Once we had our respective horses ready. Alba was staying at the Station, as we needed her horse Bonita for packing any meat that we harvested. We had planned on leaving Ripley behind with Alba, but the black German Shepard was having none of it, and as soon as we headed north, Ripley followed.

The day was overcast and there was a slight wind out of the north. It was cold, but not unpleasant. It had to be about 40 degrees.

Within an hour, we spotted 2 mule deer in a meadow next to the flowing waters of a small creek. Both Archer and I dismounted, and Archer said, "Show me what you have, kid."

Once out of the saddle, I had pulled my Henry lever action from the scabbard. Releasing Ella's reins, I then levered a 45 long colt shell into the chamber. Slowly laying down on the ground to make myself more stationary with no movement. Once comfortable and not taking my eye off of the mule deer 200 yards to the north, I brought my rifle slowly to my shoulder. Peering through the Leupold VX-Freedom Scout 1.5-4x28 scope on the rifle, and then took aim at the nearest buck. He was a magnificent looking 6 pointer, big and muscular. Once I had him in my sights. I exhaled and then slowly squeezed the trigger. The rifle shot echoed across the refuge. At first, I thought my shot had missed the big buck, for he turned and looked directly at me. Not moving, just looking at me for a full 30 seconds. Then he staggered once, then a second time. He didn't bolt like his companion did, for after the staggers his front legs buckled, and he collapsed. Archer seemed impressed when he said, "Dixon that was one hell of a shot. Let's go gut us a deer."

Once we reached the mule deer, it was obvious he was dead. Archer and I both dismounted and pulled our skinning knives.

Archer took control and started in field dressing the deer with much more skill than I had. Once again it impressed me watching Archer with his wilderness savvy. The older man was very much at home in this world of Tartarus. He was the toughest, and most capable, man I had ever known.

Once the deer was gutted, it took the both of us some man handling and muscle to get him loaded on Bonita. After that chore was completed, we sat down on a log, and Ripley laid down at my feet to take a breather. I thought now was a good time to talk to Archer about my dream. Looking at the man I admired, I said, "Archer, I got something to run by you to see what you think about it."

"I am all ears. Got nothing else on the agenda right now."

Told Archer my worries about the Holy Joe that seemed to sense we were watching him. I told him about the dream and that Alba had disappeared, and my frantic search for her in the Station's wreckage. Telling the man I respected, my fears that the Station was no longer a safe haven and that eventually the Holy Joes would return in force to take a better look at the Station.

Archer listened quietly, and after I had spoken, he sat in silence for what seemed a long time. Then he looked me in the eye, "Dixon, do you remember when, I said, - War is the remedy that our enemies have chosen? Eventually, we will be forced into giving them all they want. Do you know where Joe Spawn and his follower's compound are?"

"Not exactly. I have tried to stay clear of them as much as I could. I know it is somewhere in Brighton. They seem to congregate in that area."

Archer nodded his head in understanding, then said, "How far is Brighton from here?"

"Give or take 14 miles."

Archer took another minute to think about that, then he replied, "Dixon, we got to think about this as a war. Part of that is knowing the strength of our enemy. Right now, we are in the dark on their numbers and military capabilities. We need to survey the enemy's territory and locate them and do some reconnaissance. Determine the Holy Joes' strategic abilities. We need to make them think we are as strong as they are. We have taken out a few of their numbers, so far, we have been just a thorn in their side. But they need to understand, we do not give a rat's ass about them and that we will kill as many as it takes, no matter how long it takes. We need to dictate to them our terms. But we need information on them to do so. We need to go to Brighton."

Once we returned to the Station, Archer and I butchered the mule deer and that night we all had venison steaks with freeze-dried corn and mashed potatoes. It was a feast for kings.

After we had our bellies full of good food, Archer and I laid out our intentions to Alba for doing a reconnaissance of the Holy Joes encampment. Archer explained to Alba the need to know the strengths and the weakness of our enemy. Alba agreed that was all a great idea. Alba said she wasn't feeling well and decided to go to bed early.

For the next several hours, with the help of an old Rand McNally Road atlas, I detailed everything on the map for Archer that I knew from the Station to Brighton. Places to avoid a Gunner patrol if needed, or buildings that were large enough to put the horses into in case we ran into a severe storm.

Although it was only 14 miles to Brighton, I did not know the exact location of the Holy Joe compound. So, Archer and I planned to take enough provisions for a week. It was actually enjoyable to sit and talk to Archer about this patrol we were going to embark on. It now seemed important and the prudent thing to do.

Knowing the coming autumn and winter were close at hand, we decide the sooner the better for this patrol. Archer suggested we leave in 2 days' time. Take tomorrow to gather our gear and provisions and leave as soon as daybreak on the following day. Seemed like the perfect plan to me. The plan was for all of us to go, including Alba and Ripley.

Archer went to take his shower and turn in for the night, as I checked in on the horses one last time for the night. After giving Ella, Bonita, and Ladybird all a pinch of sugar for a treat, I bid them goodnight. I spent about 30 minutes in the security monitor room checking the exterior of the Station. I saw nothing that alarmed me and headed to go take my shower and then to join Alba in our room.

Once showered, opening the door to our room, the lights were off, but there were dancing shadows on the walls. Alba had lit a candle. The scent of black cherry from the candle was pleasing and meant only one thing. Alba was in the mood for some loving, and I was just about to get lucky. Closing the door, I moved towards the bed and Alba sat up, letting the covers fall away, exposing her to me. She was already naked, and her nipples were hard. Undressing quickly, I sat down next to the woman I loved and kissed her gently and lovingly on the lips. Breaking our embrace, I said, "I thought you were not feeling well. But here you are, in the flame's shadows waiting for me. What's up with that?"

"The last couple of days, I have not been up to snuff, but I think it is time to celebrate."

Women, it was difficult for me to understand them. Not that I had a lot of experience, but I had seen enough movies, and read enough books, to know it was the way of the world. Men are not supposed to understand women, it seems to be the law of nature. Seeing this beautiful woman naked and willing made it all seem right somehow. Leaning in closer, I had to ask the most obvious question, "What, exactly, are we celebrating?"

Alba chuckled seductively, then said, "I will tell you after we make love."

Smells of black cherry, and the sweaty aroma of each of our desires, had me deciding that Alba's timetable of telling me what we were celebrating was okay with me. Leaning in closer and feeling the heat of the moment and Alba's heartbeat, I whispered, "In that case, my love, I am in no hurry to find out what we are celebrating."

Our love making on this night seemed so perfect in every sense. There was no fumbling, and we both knew instinctively what the other desired and wanted. It was as if time stood still, and the only ones left in the world were just the 2 of us. I loved this woman like there was no tomorrow. It took a while to satisfy Alba, but when that satisfaction came, it came in wave after wave. It felt good to give her what she craved and needed.

Afterward we were both spent and exhausted from the lovemaking, we laid in bed watching the candles flame dance its shadows on the walls and the ceiling of our room for several minutes, before, I asked, "Okay babe, what exactly did we just celebrate?"

Alba rolled on her side, and she smiled for what seemed a long time before she spoke. "I am excited, but also scared to tell you."

"Well, just tell me, and I will decide which emotion we should be feeling."

Alba laid her hand on my chest so she could feel my heartbeat, which was still beating a drum after the workout it had just been through. Alba, still smiling, "I am pregnant. Dixon Mateo, you are going to be a father."

CHAPTER 18

At first Alba's words didn't sink in, and then slowly they took hold. The news of being a father actually dumbfounded me, and at first, I couldn't speak. Wasn't expecting this type of celebratory news, never thought in this world of Tartarus, that I would ever be a father. Reaching out, I brought Alba in close and held her tight, and asked, "Are you sure? How do you know?"

Alba laughed heartily and replied, "Don't be a dork, Dixon. I am a woman, I know. Don't act so surprised. It is not like we did anything to prevent it. It is the way of nature."

Peaks and valleys of emotions flowed through my body. I was happy, but nervous. I did not know how to be a good father. My father had died when I was so young. I had nothing to give me the strength, nothing to draw on for an example, or knowledge of being a wonderful dad. One thing that I felt the utmost was being elated that this woman I loved would have my child. There was doubt, of course, not so sure bringing a child into what was left of this world - was a good idea. I would have to ponder more on it in the coming days. In this moment, though, all I wanted to do was to share in the joy that was rolling out of Alba's aura. Her face was lit up like the Christmas trees in the old days. It was good to see her so happy. It made my heart smile.

We laid there in silence, holding each other, thinking our own thoughts, until Alba finally drifted off to sleep. Still awake, and from deep within the nagging memory of the dream, I had, where Alba was missing, creeped forward. The fear I felt of losing Alba, and now our baby, was almost overwhelming. The minutes passed into another hour and the black cherry candle ran out of wick and the comforting dancing firelight shadows disappeared from the walls of our room. I could not help but think it connected the disappearance of the shadows to my dream of Alba disappearing. Emotionally torn and exhausted, I finally fell asleep.

In the morning, I was groggy from lack of sleep when I felt Alba quietly slip out of bed. Without her knowing, I watched her walk across the room. She didn't look pregnant to me, but it was still early. Remembering her exuberance and the glow of her aura last night when she told me about our child was a gift that kept on giving. I would try to focus on that moment to lift my spirit and not on the eerie dream of her disappearance.

Knowing today was the day Archer had set aside to gather supplies and weapons for our reconnaissance mission to find the Holy Joe encampment. The purpose of this was to evaluate the strength and weaknesses of the Joseph Spawn disciples. Knowing Archer was probably up and about already, I slowly dragged my ass out of bed.

After a hearty breakfast of venison steak and freeze-dried eggs, Archer and I went to work on gathering supplies and ammunition for the trip to Brighton.

Alba's chore today was to feed and grain the horses. After making sure all the horses had their bellies full, she groomed Ella, Bonita, and Ladybird, combing out their manes and tails. Ripley was just a step behind Alba and stuck close to her during this time as if the German Shepard knew Alba was carrying our baby. As if Ripley knew Alba needed extra protection now.

Archer and I moved the supplies and the weapons we had decided on for the mission into the garage and barn area and were sitting them aside as Alba worked on the horses. The hardest work of the day already accomplished. We all sat down on the small loading dock in the garage to take a breather. Archer was looking at Alba and said, "You still must not be feeling well this morning. You look exhausted and should have let Dixon and I take care of the horses."

Alba smiled and returned Archer's gaze. Wiping the sweat from her forehead, "I am a tad tired today, but I need to work through this, and get used to it. I suspect it will only get worse as I gain more weight."

Archer's face had a look of puzzlement. "Gain weight?"

Alba laughed out loud, enjoying the look of total confusion on Archer's face, before she spoke, "Dixon, must have not told you yet. I am pregnant."

Archer was still muddled as Alba's words sank in, and he seemed sort of taken aback by the news of the pregnancy. He stuttered a little, before asking, "Pregnant? Like having a baby pregnant?"

Alba and I both laughed. Ripley, looking at Archer, even tilted her head as if she couldn't believe he had said that. Alba, still smiling, reached out and touched Archer's arm, and said, "Yes, we are having a baby. We would like for you to accept the responsibility of being our child's grandfather. If that suits you, we would love for you to be part of the child's life. Dixon and I have learned to rely on you for your knowledge and wisdom. We want you to be a part of this, especially now, in this world of Tartarus that we find ourselves. What do you say, big guy?"

I had not seen Archer ever baffled or confused, and I sure as hell never dreamed that the man would tear up. There is a first for everything. Archer's eyes got misty, and a tear formed and rolled down his face as he took a moment to gather his thoughts. His eyes never left Albas, and as Archer was thinking on what to say, Alba smiled, and her tears started to roll. I probably had never seen in my life such a magical moment as this. It affected me so that I teared up.

Archer finally reached out and pulled Alba into his arms and pressed her against his chest, then he spoke. "I always wanted a family. A Norman Rockwell type of family, a dog, a white picket fence, a house in the country. Love of children and of grandchildren. I almost achieved that. Maria, my exquisite wife, and I before she died, came close but failed in one department. We wanted kids, but the good Lord never blessed us with the opportunity. I had not been so blessed until I met you and Dixon. Being a family means you are a part of something very wonderful. It means you will love and be loved for the rest of your life. Yes, yes, I would love to be a part of Dixon and your baby's life. I am honored that you ask me to be part of the baby's future. It makes my heart sing."

With the news of the new addition in our lives, the rest of the day seemed almost jovial as we continued to prepare for the reconnaissance mission north into what was left of the city of Brighton and the stronghold of Joe Spawn and his Holy Joe's disciples. We decided since Alba was not feeling well, that she would stay behind. I had mixed feelings about that. Alba would be alone, with no backup, until we got back home to the Station. The town of Brighton was only 14 miles, but we did not know where exactly the Holy Joe compound might be. Archer was confident that we would find it in a day or so. He wanted to spend a full day of observation of the Holy Joe encampment to get a handle on what their strengths and weaknesses were. Then the trip back. If all went well, we should be back at the Station in 4-6 days.

Alba handles herself well and kept herself alive before I rescued her from the pack of wild dogs. She was tougher than me in some ways, absolutely smarter than me. I kept telling myself that she should be fine. But now with the baby, and the memory of the dream I had, I was bothered by the prospect of her being alone for that much time.

The next morning, after Ella, Bonita, and Ladybird were packed for the trail north, I kissed Alba goodbye. Our kissed lingered for a long time and I had the feeling that Alba might even regret that we were leaving her behind. Archer, mounted on Ladybird, was getting impatient and was ready for this new adventure, so I pushed all my misgivings back to the dark corners of my mind. As we started north towards the Wildlife refuge. I looked back over my shoulders at Alba as she waved goodbye to us. I was overwhelmed with a sense of dread that something was not right, that something in our world was out of kilter. A shiver of fear ran up my spine. Nothing is more frightening than a fear you cannot name.

Archer reined Ladybird around and he came back to me and said in a fatherly tone, "Dixon, quit lollygagging, you need to get your head out of the clouds and into the game. We are riding into hostile territory. The best thing you can do is have your mind right about this mission, so you can get back to that beautiful woman of yours. She will be fine. She is tougher than the 2 of us put together."

Bowman was right, of course, about everything he had said. I gave Ella some spur with Ripley keeping pace with us. I trotted past Archer, and smiled when I said, "You are right. I better take point since you are an old man Grandpa Archer."

Archer and Ladybird started to trot, and when he caught up with Ella and me, he smiled then said, "I think Grandpa Archer sounds just about right. Since you are the youngster, you do need to take point and relieve this old man of such duty."

Approaching from the south on Highway 85, by noon we were within 2 miles of Brighton, Colorado town limit. The family produce and truck farms were on the southern edge of town. We were riding past what used to be Johnson Auto Plaza, a Jeep and Chrysler dealer. I spent a lot of money at this auto dealer repairing and buying parts for my Jeep Liberty and Dodge Charger. There were several what used to be brand new Jeep Rubicon's collecting dust in the parking lot in front of the showroom. Before Tartarus, they were my dream vehicle. Always wanted one, but the sticker price at the time was a shocker and I could not afford them. Now the free for the taking price was right, but there was no gasoline to be had. Such was my luck. Looking away from Johnson Plaza and turning my attention to the east, not a quarter of a mile from here is where I had been shot and wounded over a sack of sweet corn.

Archer thought the center and downtown would have long been abandoned. He reasoned that the Holy Joe compound would be close to the old truck farms for the simple need to grow food for any large community. It sounded reasonable to me. We headed east off of Highway 85 and followed 136th Avenue, looking for any sign of human activity. We rode the horses through what used to be the old truck farms before Tartarus.

We would rely heavily on Ella, Bonita, Ladybird and especially Ripley to give us warning of danger. I knew she was more than up to that task. Ripley, without being told, took point and had moved up about 30 yards in front, giving us the best chance of knowing when there was a threat close by.

The pavement of 136th Avenue was potholed and in a sad state of disrepair. With the weather swinging towards the winter months, the abundant weeds that had grown in the gaping holes in the road had withered and died. Road construction and the maintenance of the roads had long ago disappeared. Seeing the road in such a deteriorated condition showed that with the rapid decline of civilization, how quickly nature was reclaiming its own.

The clouds in the north that had darkened shortly after leaving the Station, were now overhead. Clouds now above our heads looked as if they could and would rain at any moment. Temperature had dropped and the breeze streaming from the north had increased as the storm clouds had moved in. The weather had cast the gloom of the impending winter upon this day. That gloom matched my disposition. I was still uneasy about leaving Alba all alone back home at the Station.

To the north of us was the old "Berry Patch Farm". Back when I was a kid, it was a great place to buy fresh produce, such as lettuce, cucumbers, strawberries, corn, cabbage, tomatoes, and potatoes. I remember going there with my parents, thinking how boring it was. Oh, how I wished to have those days back now. I stopped to look at the old and depleted sign. Berry Patch Farms painted name on the old sign had faded, cracked, and was peeling away. The left pillar had rotted away and could no longer support the heavy wooden sign, the sign was now sitting cockeyed. The left corner was firmly planted to the ground and the right side was still supported by the right pillar. Would not be long, just like the rest of humanity, before it all collapsed.

Archer and Lady Bird, with Bonita reined to Ladybird's saddle was trailing behind, when they had caught up with me. Archer then asked, "Anything the matter?"

I pointed towards the old sign, and then said, "No, just remembering when I used to go here with my parents. Just feeling a little nostalgic is all."

"I get that way sometimes myself. But we need to keep moving."

We started moving eastward again. Monitoring Ripley, I saw her stop, then crouched low to the ground, looking northeast. Then she stood up and hightailed it back to our position. Something was ahead, and she had just alerted us to the potential danger. There was an old horse barn that had seen better days just to our left and north of 136th Avenue. I pointed towards the barn and Archer nodded his head in an affirmative. We reined the horses towards the barn and gave them some spur. Ripley had already figured out that was our destination and she actually beat us there.

Once inside the weathered barn, we tied off the horses, then took our rifles out of the scabbards and checked to see if they were fully loaded. Once satisfied with that, we checked our pistols. We were ready to fight if need be. Pulling our field glasses out of the saddlebags, we moved to the rear doors and exited the barn. Staying in the shadows and partially hidden by some old rotting hay bales, we surveyed the area that Ripley had showed.

Archer was the first that saw it and pointed, and then said, "I got movement."

Moving my binoculars to where Archer had showed and focused in on it. After several seconds, I said, "I got it as well. It is a lone man walking in our directions."

Archer added, "Good news is, he is walking as if he does not have a care in the world. He didn't see Ripley or us. He doesn't know we are here."

CHAPTER 19

Archer, after several more seconds, "He is a youngster, and looks to be carrying one of those ancient rifles, an ArmaLite AR-15."

"I concur. I had heard and read stories about those rifles being the go-to weapon for psychos in mass shootings before Tartarus. Never seen one in person, just photos in magazines. Nor do I know anything about the fire capabilities of the rifle."

Archer, with his binoculars still on the man walking towards us, "The original AR-15 is a select-fire, gas-operated, air-cooled, magazine-fed rifle. The ArmaLite AR-15 was designed to be a lightweight rifle and to fire a high-velocity, lightweight, small-caliber cartridge to allow infantrymen to carry more ammunition. Ammo for the rifle is a 223 Remington. The way this fellow is carrying his weapon, he seems to be unfamiliar with it."

Once again, I was amazed at Archer Bowman's knowledge. There was more to the man than I knew. The way he talked, his intelligence, his demeanor, was telling of Archer being more than just a brother that somehow survived the death of humanity and became old. He was a warrior from long ago. Alba, the new baby, and I were lucky to have him in our family, our clan.

As the man walking got closer, it became clear who he was. Viewing him, a few more seconds to be sure, then I said, "He is wearing the cleric collar of the Holy Joes. He is one of Joe Spawn's boys."

I could hear Archer chuckle slightly, before he said, "I wonder how we got so lucky?"

"Lucky?"

"Hell, yes, Dixon my boy; lucky. We were searching for the Holy Joe compound, and out of nowhere, a travel guide just appeared to help our cause."

Thinking about that, I said, "How do we know he will take us to the compound?"

Without dropping his binoculars, Archer replied, "That fellow is young, and probably stupid, and he will fear for his life. We are going to scare the shit out of that boy. He will give us the location and take us there. I guarantee it."

Knowing Archer, I had no doubt he would make the young man talk. We watched for another 5 minutes until he was almost next to the old barn. Archer whispered, "This is how we play this. You and Ripley walk out slowly with your EBR to the shoulder and pointed at him. I will be a step behind and move in from his side. If he tries to bolt to the south, sic Ripley on him. Try not to shoot him. We need him alive."

Scanning with my field glasses behind the walking man, seeing nothing, I said, "Sounds like a plan to me. We are clear all the way around. He is alone."

Crouching behind the rotted stack of hay bales, Archer indicated with hand signals that when I approached the Holy Joe, he would move around the other side of the hay and then make his appearance. Watching Archer, he finally gave me the hand signal to move on the Joe Spawn man. Standing slowly, I moved forward with Ripley at my side towards the Holy Joe. The man was lost in thought apparently and did not notice Ripley or me until we were in his line of sight. Pointing my EBR at his head, the man at first seemed confused, then slowly I could see the fear overtake his eyes, as he realized the danger, he was in. Never once did he try to raise his weapon. He obviously did not have any survival or military training. Ripley moved instinctively to the south, cutting the Holy Joe off if he ran for it. Speaking in a clear voice, I said, "We do not want to harm you or shoot you, but I will need you to slowly lay down your AR-15 to the ground in front of you."

The Holy Joe's eyes kept darting back and forth in between me and Ripley as if he was trying to comprehend if he was going to die or not. Then he saw Archer move in closer to his left. But the Holy Joe just stood there doing nothing. Archer spoke up, "Son, your situational awareness really sucks. Do as the man say and lay down your weapon. We do not want to shoot you."

This Holy Joe now looked on the verge of tears, and I was hoping he would do nothing stupid. He finally gave into his situation and slowly laid the AR-15 down at his feet.

As Archer moved in while I covered him, the Holy Joe said something that surprised the both of us. "I don't have any ammo for it, anyway."

Archer retrieved the AR-15, and then quickly searched our new prisoner. When Archer was satisfied the Holy Joe had no other weapons, he nodded at me, and I lowered my rifle. I walked up to the young man and said, "My name is Dixon." Pointing at Archer, I continued, "His name is Archer, and the dog's name is Ripley. What is your name?"

The young man was very skinny and stood about 5'7". His clothes were dirty, tattered, and worn. His scraggly brown hair was down to his shoulders and looked as if had not been washed in a decade or so. The young Holy Joe looked genuinely surprised we had not shot him and were being cordial to him. His voice stuttered when he spoke. "Russ, my name is Russ Papp. Do you have anything to eat?"

I looked towards Archer, and he looked a tad baffled. Then he shrugged his shoulders as if, just like me, he had not expected our new prisoner to be taken so easily. Looking back at Russ, "I said, yes, we got some food. We got some freeze-dried pot roast stew, or freeze-dried macaroni and cheese. We will feed you, then we have several questions to ask you."

Russ's face lit up with a huge smile, knowing he was going to get some chow. Then, this time without a stutter, he said, "Dixon, thank you. They both sound so good. Can I have both?"

Looking towards Archer, once again Archer still seemed confused, but he shrugged his shoulders. Replying to Russ, "Yes, you can have both, as long as you answer our questions."

Russ Papp, the Holy Joe soldier of the radical Joseph Spawn, stuck out his hands to be handcuffed or tied. He seemed to be happy we had taken him prisoner. Especially by someone that will feed him.

Archer stepped up and spoke to the prisoner, "Russ, if you promise not to run, we will not tie your hands. Hard to eat with your hands tied up, anyway."

"No sir, I will not run. You caught me fair and square."

Russ's statement almost made me laugh out loud. It was obvious we would not have to scare the shit out of our prisoner, as Archer originally thought we would have to do. All we had to do was show a little kindness and feed him. Russ Papp seemed to be simpleminded and did not seem to be as radical as the Holy Joes we had encountered before. Especially those we had fought at the Walmart. I was curious to hear his story. Putting my hand gently on Russ's shoulder, I said, "Now that we got that all cleared up that you will not hightail it out of here. Let's get you some grub."

We started back to the old, abandoned barn, and Russ happily followed us. It would seem we had a new friend. Ripley, who had been standing off to the side during the capture of Russ, now walked slowly up to the captured Holy Joe. Russ reached out and started petting Ripley, which Ripley favorably accepted. It would seem Ripley had stamped her approval on the Holy Joe. Ripley was always an excellent judge of character.

Since Archer and I had not eaten yet, we set up both camp stoves we brought, to boil water. I fixed the first pot roast stew for Russ and handed it to him. He gulped it down as if he had not eaten in a while. Archer ate his meal as I prepared a package of freeze-dried macaroni and cheese for Russ. I asked him, "Russ, how old are you?"

Russ stopped and looked skyward, as if he was trying to remember, then he smiled before replying. "I turned 19 last week."

Russ Papp had been born after the world had succumbed to Tartarus and he would have never known any difference in how the world used to be. Realizing this made me sad for the young man. Once the macaroni and cheese was ready, I handed the package to Russ. As I was doing so, I pointed to the cleric collar he was wearing and asked, "What's up with the collar?"

Before answering, Russ dug into the mac and cheese and between bites, he said, "Reverend Spawn, makes all that belong to the temple wear them."

Making 2 more packages of freeze-dried pot roast stew, one for Ripley and one for myself, Archer took over the questioning of Russ. Archer asked, "Temple? Do you live there?"

Russ had his belly full, and he actually seemed very cheerful at the moment, as he answered Archer's question. "The Temple is everything. It is where we all live. There are several buildings. Yes, I live at the temple with the chosen people. The ones that the Reverend says God has blessed to be his soldiers. I have always lived there. Although I do not feel like the others, I don't feel like God has chosen me for anything in particular. Reverend Spawn does not like or trust me about anything. He makes me so angry sometimes. The only reason he let me live there is that my mom is his main wife. The other men, the chosen ones, will not give me any bullets for my gun, which is why I didn't have any. I have never shot my rifle, don't know how. Most of the others at the temple make fun of me and call me stupid. They barely give me anything to eat. I have to wait until everyone else is done eating, then I get their scraps of food. I hate living there."

Ripley and I finished our dinner as we listened to Russ Papp. No wonder the kid was so skinny and asked for food. His meal today must have seemed like a feast to someone such as him. Archer continues with his questioning, "So, your mom is the Reverend's wife? Are you, his son?"

Russ looked down at that ground as if he was ashamed before answering, "No, the Reverend shot my dad when I was a kid. He claimed my dad had never been a chosen one and that he should have died during the rapture. He took my mom as one of his wives. Wasn't long she was his main wife. She bosses all the other wives around. They all are scared of her."

Archer asked, "How many wives does the Reverend Spawn have?"

Russ thought about that for a few seconds before he answered, "Including my mom, he has. I think a lot."

Archer realizing, he would not get a number on how many wives, he moved on to the next question, "Russ, where is the temple located? How far away is it?"

Russ didn't even try to hide the whereabouts of the temple. He pointed northeast and said, "The temple is at the Kings. Takes me about an hour to walk there from here."

Archer's face went blank when he said, "Kings?"

I knew exactly what and where Russ was talking about, and it made perfect sense to me. Looking at Archer, "I think he means King Soopers. It is the old grocery store that my family used to shop at. Close to 2 miles from here. One parking lot that gave you access to several buildings. A strip mall with the largest store being the grocery store. In the strip mall building there was a liquor store, a phone store, a Subway, a Mexican restaurant, and a pizza joint. As I recall, there were 2 other buildings served by the parking lot, an IHOP restaurant and UPS store."

Russ just nodded his head in approval, as I was explaining the location of the Holy Joe compound to Archer. Watching the young man, my heart was breaking. I could sense his loneliness. He had connected in a short time to Ripley, Archer and I, just because we gave him a decent meal. In his simple way, he was just trying to be helpful. My sense was Russ Papp was genuinely a good person, and his heart was truly caring. Turning my attention only towards Russ, I asked, "Is the temple guarded? How many guards? How many folks live at the temple? Is there a wall or fence surrounding it?"

Ripley walked over and put her head on Russ's lap, which brought a huge smile as Russ with enthusiasm petted her. Russ eyes got bigger, before he spoke, "Yes, there are lots of guards, a lot of people, mean ones. They push me around all the time. There is a fence, no wall."

I was not going to get a straight answer on the number of guards or people at the temple, not that Russ was hiding anything. I believed he had no concept of what I was asking, so I moved on to the next question, "The fence is it a chain-link fence?"

Russ face went blank before he replied, "I don't know what that is."

"Is the fence metal or wood?"

Russ smiled, knowing the answer. "It is metal. You can see through it."

It would seem that the Holy Joe compound was fortified with a chain-link fence and guards. "Russ, do the guards have dogs?"

Russ nodded his head—no, before he spoke. "Reverend Spawn will let no one keep dogs. He says they are soulless and should not be in his place of worship. There was one once, which the soldiers had. They kept it in a secret place away from the temple. They went on patrol, and only one man returned. I never saw the dog after that."

The lone dog must have been the one I had killed at the feed store when it attacked me. Any man such as Spawn that didn't like dogs was a strange one in my book, but it was good news for us if we ever tried to make a move on the compound. We would not have to deal with any canines.

Archer spoke up, "Russ, what exactly are you doing, out here walking all by yourself?"

Russ seemed confused by the question. Then he smiled as an answer formulated in his mind. "The guards call it the Russ patrol. I am supposed to walk back and forth to the Johnsons."

The Johnsons must mean the Jeep dealership. I asked, "What do you do on this patrol? What is your duty?"

Russ once again was baffled before he replied, "Not sure what duty is. They tell me to walk, and I just walk."

Sending this young man on a worthless patrol just to be rid of him for the day. Sending him out in the world of Tartarus all alone with an empty rifle and no way to defend himself was heartless. "Russ, a couple more questions if you don't mind? When will you be missed? What time do the guards expect you back at the temple?"

Russ knew the answer to that one without thinking too much. "They never know when I get back. Sometimes, I sleep at the Johnsons if I can find food. I go back to the temple when I get hungry."

CHAPTER 20

Russ seemed blissful to be here with us, and Ripley was happy she had a new buddy to give her love. Archer pointed at me and then away from Russ. It would seem he wanted to talk to me alone without the young Holy Joe hearing what he wanted to talk about. I was pretty sure whatever Archer had to say that Russ Papp would not understand the meaning of his words, but just to be safe, I spoke to the young man, "Russ, not sure if you have figured it out yet, but Ripley loves to have the back of her ears gently massaged."

Russ, for several seconds, seemed confused. Then he realized what I had said, and a huge smile split his face as he went to massaging Ripley's ears. And by the way Ripley had moved in and laid her head back down again on Russ's lap, she was indeed loving her new friend.

Archer walked up to me and as we turned to walk away from Russ and Ripley, Archer chuckled and said, "Very good tactical diversion, distracting Russ with Ripley."

Once we thought we were far enough away from the Holy Joe, Archer told me what was on his mind. "What little conversation we have had with Russ really confirms what I think we both had already decided. That the so-called Holy Joes is a cult, and that Joseph Spawn is the absolute cult leader. Spawn has to rank right up there with some of the more famous ones, such as, Marshall Applewhite, Bhagwan Shree Rajneesh, Charles Manson, David Koresh, and my personal favorite nut job, Jim Jones." Pointing at Russ Papp, he continued, "Although not evident in this one, but the ones that you and I have crossed paths with before Russ, had the number one trait of a cult, being opposed to critical thinking outside of their faction. The second trait is that Spawn obviously seeks inappropriate loyalty to him and him only. Third trait is that Joseph Spawn has separated himself for any orthodox religion, emphasizing his own personal doctrines outside scripture. The fourth trait is that the reverend has crossed biblical boundaries of behavior, such as sexual purity and personal ownership. The fifth trait is that Spawn, by having multiple wives, he has dishonored the family unit, and as ostracized his chief wife's son, just solely on the fact that the boy is more simple-minded than most. Sixth trait is the big one, by murdering Russ's true father, Spawn has justified killing to suit his own personal agenda and beliefs. You wrap all of that up into a gift-wrapped package. What we have here is a very dangerous man with believers that are just as dangerous. The Temple, as young Russ calls it, is a formidable foe, and most assuredly a cult."

Everything that Archer had put into words was exactly what I had already assumed a long time ago. But after hearing Archer voice his thoughts, it made me realize how truly dangerous someone like Spawn could be in this new world of Tartarus. With no means to police or take down someone like Joseph Spawn, who was out of control, he could make what was left of the entire world into his own kingdom on earth. There would be no way for any of us to really predict the behavior of such a man. It was really scary thinking that Archer, Alba, Ripley, and I were living only 14 miles away from such a madman.

Looking back at Russ and Ripley, one could not help, but see the contrast of such a good and gentle person, such as Ripley's new friend, compared to his stepfather. Turning my attention back to Archer, "I could not agree more with what you just said. The problem I see, is that we have 2 questions we need to ask ourselves. What are we going to do about Joseph Spawn? And, in my mind, the most important question of the moment is, what are we going to do with Russ Papp?"

Archer looked back at Russ and stood there for several seconds, and I could see that he was in deep thought. Having thought about it, he said, "First thing is we cannot send him back to Reverend Spawn prior to our reconnaissance of the Holy Joe Temple and compound at the old King Soopers grocery store. He would give us up without thinking about it, not that he would mean to, but look how easy he gave us the information about the Temple. I say we rest until dark, and then we take the kid with us and do what we set out to do when we came here. We survey the lair of our enemy looking for their strengths and weaknesses."

I nodded my head in understanding then Archer and I moved back closer to Russ, and Archer asked the stepson of the cult leader a question, "Russ, do you know how to ride? Have you ever ridden a horse?"

Russ was so busy petting Ripley it took him almost an entire minute to answer the question, "Horses like me, and I know how to ride horses. Do you want me to show you?"

Russ seemed so confidant, it made me smile. I was hoping we were not setting him up to get hurt. In the short time that Russ had been our so-called prisoner, I had grown to like the young boy. And if push came to shove, Archer would admit he had grown a soft spot for the young Holy Joe as well.

Archer nodded at me, and as I was getting Bonita, Alba's horse ready, Archer said to Russ, "We are going to let you try to ride our spare horse to see how you do. Her name is Bonita."

Russ jumped up so fast that Archer and I instinctively started reaching for our weapons, but Russ only had eyes for Bonita. Then one of the strangest things that I had ever seen Bonita do, not even with Alba, bonita started moving towards Russ Papp and then laid her head on his shoulder. Russ was all grins as he leaned in, touching Bonita with his chest. The horse and the young Holy Joe hugged as if they were in a lover's embrace. Just like Ripley, Bonita was drawn to the young man. Animals knew a good heart and soul. And apparently Russ Papp was one of those. It would seem that animal's, no matter what type of animal, was instinctively drawn to him, as the young man was to them. Russ obviously had a gift. Archer was just as dumbfounded as I was with Bonita's reaction to Russ, and he chuckled and said, "Dixon, what we are witnessing here is the real Doctor Dolittle in the flesh."

Russ heard Archer's statement and was baffled by it. Then the young man grinned like he didn't really understand the reference to Doctor Dolittle, and said, "Doctor, oh no. Not smart enough to be a doctor. I thought I told you; I am Russ - Russ Papp."

Shaking my head in wonderment, I said, "Yes, you are Russ. The one and only Russ Papp. Let's see if you can ride Bonita now."

Russ, realizing I had just given him permission to mount up on Bonita, he did so with the grace of a very seasoned rider. Once his butt was planted in the saddle, he was grinning from ear to ear. While holding the reins, he gently reached down and rubbed Bonita's neck. Russ glanced in my direction to see if it was okay to take Bonita for a spin. Once I nodded my approval, Russ gave Bonita some soft boot, and off to the races they went. Bonita with the young Holy Joe were headed at a full trot towards Johnson's Plaza, and it was something to see. Archer and I were both amazed at the kids handling of Bonita, like all he had ever done was ride that horse. I said to Archer, "No doubt, that boy probably can't drive a car, but he sure as hell, can ride like the wind."

Bonita and Russ didn't slow down and kept moving down the road. They were getting far enough away that they were getting harder and harder to see. That is when Archer laughingly remarked, "Shit, do you think Russ realizes he needs to come back?"

Watching Russ ride away into the western horizon, I started laughing at what Archer had said. It had been a pleasant surprise all the way around in the capture of Russ Papp. I answered the question. "He will be back when he gets hungry. The kid likes our chow."

It was only a minute later that Russ and Bonita appeared on the horizon in the west and were headed eastward, back in our direction. They were no longer at a trot. They both must have gotten the vigor out of their system and were slowly making their way back to our position. Archer's face split in two with a grin, as he stated, "We best get some water boiling to make some grub. Russ will be hungry after that ride. We will put the feed bags on, eat, then wait until it gets dark, then we will make our way to the Holy Joe compound."

"Sounds like a plan." Watching Archer look in the distance at Russ. It would seem the old man had found someone that made him remember. Tartarus had destroyed not all of humanity. Russ Papp was an example of that. Regardless of his upbringing and the hardships he had faced, in all the adversity that the young man had endured, he was a genuinely good person, with an obvious heart of gold.

It wasn't long before Russ and Bonita made it back to the old barn. Russ once again amazed me. Without being told to do so, he unsaddled Bonita and started caring for her like he had owned her forever. In that short time that the Bonita and Russ had spent together, they had bonded. Just like Ripley had bonded with the young man. Just like Archer and I were bonding with Russ. It was refreshing and invigorating to me to feel this way.

After brushing Bonita's mane and tail out with a wooden curry comb, I had given Russ, he then let the mare join Ella and Ladybird as they grazed in the tall grass just to the south of the old abandon barn. Russ never took his eyes off of Bonita, it was evident that he had fallen in love with Alba's horse. I knew that Alba's heart would rejoice in this.

As the sun was finally dropping behind the mountains to the west, the orange, blue hue of the encroaching night made its appearance. We all settled down and had a freeze-dried supper of spaghetti and meat sauce. The grub was filling, and it tasted okay, but I missed the days from long ago when my mom used to make her pasta sauce from scratch.

Russ had settled in a spot on an old hay bale to eat his supper, Ripley glued herself to the leg of her new best friend. Russ was obviously enjoying not only the food, but the company of Bonita, Ripley, Archer, and me. Once he finished his supper, in an innocent, almost childlike voice, Russ spoke. "Can I go with you? I can do chores and take care of Ripley and the horses."

If that didn't pull at my heartstrings, nothing would. In the short time that Russ had been our "prisoner," we had made an impression on the young man. On the other side of that coin, he had made an impression on me. I was sort of taken aback by Russ's question. The stepson of Reverend Spawn had a heartfelt yearning of wanting to belong some place that treated him as a human, as an equal. I wasn't sure how to respond. Looking at Archer, who was only looking at Russ, I saw a tear glisten in his eye. Russ's question had also touched Archer Bowman, the last surviving brother of 3. After a full minute Archer said, "If Dixon and I decided to take you back to where we came from, you would no longer see your mother, the Temple, or any of the folks you grew up with. Is that something you had thought about?"

Russ didn't even hesitate when he answered, "Sometimes the place you live, the place you are used to, is not the place you belong."

Oh, my God, there it was. The unassuming, genuine wholehearted answer to a very complicated question. In the mind of this young, and simple boy was the wisdom of an aged philosopher. Russ had more insight into himself at such a young age than most people have in themselves in an entire lifetime. Those at the Holy Joe compound could have, should have, taken the time to listen and learn from such an amazing young man. Archer and I both looked at one another and at the same time, we both shrugged our shoulders in defeat. Without a word spoken, and without Alba knowing, Archer and I, just added another to our clan of misfits.

CHAPTER 21

Archer stood up and walked over to Russ and sat down next to him on the hay bale. He looked the young man straight in the eye and said, "Leaving the Temple and your mom. I want you to think really hard about that, and you need to decide if that is what you really want to do."

Once again, Russ, being Russ, did not hesitate. "I will not miss the bad things. My mom, she hates me, she says I remind her of my dad. Reverend Spawn has never liked me, and the other chosen ones make fun of me and call me dumb. But you know what, Mr. Archer? I respect myself enough to walk away from those that hurt me and want to be me. I want to be Russ, Russ Papp. Felt like I was waiting on something good that was going to happen, and it never did. Being captured by you and Mr. Dixon feels good. It feels like I belong. I think now this is what I was always waiting for."

I stood up and walked closer to Russ, and spoke to him, "Archer, and I had already decided if you wanted to come and stay with us, that you are more than welcome to do so. I need to tell you I have a wife named Alba. And we are going to have a baby soon."

Russ grinned from ear to ear and said, "Alba, I like that name. Alba is so pretty. New baby? Can I be an uncle? Uncle Russ, Russ Papp?"

This kid made me smile, with his enthusiasm at hearing Alba's name, and on wanting to be an uncle. Trying not to chuckle, I said, "Our new baby got a Grandpa Archer, and now he has an Uncle Russ. Yes, you can be Uncle Russ Papp."

Russ jumped up so fast it startled me, and he rushed forward and hugged me. It all happened so fast; I was not sure how to respond. I glanced at Archer, and he was trying very hard to control his laughter. Russ was definitely going to make life at the station very interesting.

As soon as the sun disappeared, and when the night creeped in, the air had gotten chilly, and I could see my breath, I could smell the last nights of autumn dancing in the breeze. We had all hunkered down trying to stay warm, waiting for the half-moon to reach the pinnacle of the night. We had decided to let the folks at the Temple compound to settle in and get sleepy before we moved in to check out our adversary's encampment.

Russ and Archer had fallen asleep, since I was the one that we decided on to stay awake and guard the camp. Watching the half-moon rise in the east, as it leisurely made its way to be straight overhead, reminded me of how things were before Tartarus, and especially my mom. My mom had a fascination with the moon, and she would take every chance that she could to pass on that passion and her knowledge on the subject to me. It was my mom that told me that the half-moon was called Luna, or sickle of the moon, also waning and waxing moon. The Luna is a sign of fertility, related to life and death, and thus a popular symbol in many religions. It pinpoints changing seasons, ebb and tide (and related inundations as harbingers of fertility), and the feminine menstrual cycle. It was at times such as this, when all alone and looking at the moon, I rejoiced in my memories of the woman that gave me life.

Once I determined it was about midnight, I woke up Archer first. Archer stood up and stretched, getting the kinks out, and told me, "I will hustle up the horses while you get Russ awake."

I stepped over and gently shook Russ, and said, "Time to get up Russ, Russ Papp." Shit, the kid had me saying it like he did.

Russ got up quickly and was shaking off his sleep when Archer showed up with all 3 horses in tow. Archer said to Russ, "Remember, we are going to let you show us the compound, but we have to do it on the sly. Those in the Temple must never know we were there."

Russ grabbed Bonita's reins and before he mounted the mare, he said, "I know a quick way across the fields. We should stay off the roads in case the others are coming back."

Took me a second to understand what Russ had just said. Once it settled into my mind I asked, "What others? What are you talking about?"

Russ then said, "The chosen ones went on a patrol the night before to C-City."

That got Archer and my attention. I asked, "C-City? You mean Commerce City?"

Russ, without hesitation, answered, "Yes, went to C-City. The police station in C-City."

Archer said it before me, "Shit, they are headed to the station! And Alba does not know they are coming!"

The worse feeling is trying to hold back a panic attack when faced with uncertain situations. I had never had an attack, but I felt as if I was straddling the fence with one right now. I felt someone had tilted my world off of its axis with what Russ had revealed. The reoccurring dream I had been having about Alba's disappearance was now looking as if it had been a premonition of events that had not happened yet. I was not sure how I could face this world of Tartarus without Alba and the baby. Looking at Archer, I said, "We need to leave now and head back home."

Archer's face, I know, mirrored my own, in our worry and fears about Alba, so much in fact that he didn't even hesitate. "I agree. The horses are ready, and we need to hit the trail now."

Once I had planted my butt in the saddle on Ella, I reined her head around towards the south when Archer yelled, "Hold on! Hold on!" Archer was already mounted on Ladybird, but now he pointed at Russ, then said, "Russ, the Holy Joes, and the ones you call the Chosen Ones, are headed to our home in Commerce City. Dixon's wife, Alba, probably is in serious danger. If you want to go with us, now is the time to decide and we cannot waste another minute. It is now or never!"

Even before Archer had finished his last sentence, Russ had already gotten himself saddled up on Bonita, and he said, "Russ, Russ Papp goes to C-City with his friends!"

With nothing more to add to the conversation, I gave Ella some spur and all of us headed south into the darkness of the night.

Pushing the horses hard into the chilled air, that was only getting colder as the night progressed. There were no clouds to blanket in the heat of the day, but there was a full moon overhead to give us the best lighting we could hope for riding the trail at night.

I had slept none in the last 24 hours, and I needed to quit using all my energy worrying about Alba and the baby. Worrying and the lack of sleep could cause me to make mistakes and right now, none of us could afford me making blunders. Any slipup on my part could be a fatal one for those I care about and love. I said a silent prayer that Alba had hidden when the Holy Joes had appeared at the station. I had to believe that she was okay and waiting for us to return.

Halfway home, with 7 miles left on the trek back to the Station and Alba, Archer pulled Ladybird to a halt. Since he had been in the front and on point for our journey back home, it forced Russ and me to come to a halt just behind him. Archer spun Ladybird in a circle in front of us, calming his horse down. He said to Russ and me, "We need to take a breather. We are pushing the horses too hard."

Without thinking, I quickly replied, "Hell no Archer! We need to keep going! We cannot waste any time!"

Archer rode up to me, so we were side by side. Archer, in a calming voice, said, "Dixon, you are being reactionary to the events that are unfolding, and not thinking straight. Listen to me, son, my worries about Alba and the baby are the same as yours. But we have to reason this out. Whatever was going to happen at the station, has already happened. Killing our horses to get there will not prevent that." Leaning in closer to look into my eyes, Archer continued, "We need to rest the horses now. Give them something to drink and not push them any harder after we regain the trail. I know that does not seem like the prudent thing to do in your mind, but hear me out. Whatever we find at the Station, is going to be one of 3 things. Number 1, we find her safe and sound, number 2, is we find her dead, number 3, is the Holy Joes have taken her prisoner. If number 1 is what the reality is, then we did not injure ourselves or the horses in the push to get to the Station. If we find that number 2 or 3 is what the reality is, then we will need fresh horses to go back to the Holy Joe compound to either rescue Alba or kill every son of a bitch there!"

"I hate when you are right! But I admit you are right, and we will do as you say. Just promise me Archer, if they have hurt Alba in any shape or form, that we are going back to exact justice on those that have caused her harm!"

Archer reached out and touched my shoulder, then said, "That I can do, my friend! I swear to you if any harm has come to Alba, I will give my life seeking retribution! There will be a reckoning the Holy Joes will never see coming!"

The next hour was the longest hour of my life. Russ Papp proved to be the person both Archer, and I believed him to be. Once we stopped, and without being asked to do so, he went about taking care of the horses by giving each some water from our canteens, then showing them love by using a curry comb on their manes and tails. The horses seemed to trust the young man just like Ripley had.

Ripley had kept up with the horses as we pushed them hard for the first 7 miles back to the Station. She was now sound asleep, conserving energy for the last 7 miles. Sleeping is what I should do, but my stomach was all knotted up. I spent the time cleaning and checking my weapons, making sure I was ready for any confrontation with the Holy Joes.

Archer had asked Russ on what roads the Holy Joes would have used as they headed to Commerce City or headed back towards Brighton. We hoped we would run into their patrol. Russ did not know since he had never been allowed to go to C-City. When we had headed to Brighton, the Holy Joes had been headed to the Station, and we never crossed trails with them. So, the chances of crossing trails with them now were slim to none. If we did, it would be just pure chance.

After sufficient time for the horses to rest, Archer, Russ and I mounted up, and with Ripley by my side, we continued on into the night at a slower pace to save the horses strength in case we had to turn around and come right back.

The night had gotten considerably colder, and I could see Ella's breath as she exhaled. The thousands numbered the stars above. When the city lights years ago had finally gone out for good, the stars on a cloudless night had no competition for dominance of the night sky. Tonight, especially, they seemed brighter than normal as they rained their illuminance down upon us. If not for the dire circumstance of what may have happened at the Station, I would have stopped and observed the beauty of the light show in the heavens. But there was no time, and we kept moving south towards home through the dark.

Even after riding all night with no sleep in over 24 hours, I was not tired. The adrenaline was still pumping through my body. I could not sleep without knowing what had happened to Alba.

There was a faint line of orange on the eastern horizon as the sun was now trying to raise its sleepy head and drive the darkness away. One can only appreciate the miracle of a sunrise if you have waited in the darkness. This sunrise had almost perfect timing with our approach to the Station. It would give us the much-needed light to observe the Station before we reached it. But it would also be early enough if the Holy Joes, had decided not to travel at night that they might still be asleep. If they were still at the Station, I knew we would be outnumbered and outgunned, so I would welcome any advantage we had.

We approached the Station from the Rocky Mountain Arsenal. It provided better cover, and I knew of a stand of trees that we could stop at and use for cover to observe. If the Holy Joes were still there, we would need to know how many there would be against us if it came to a shooting match.

The sun had just cleared the horizon and there was a brilliant orange hue cast upon the landscape just as we reached the stand of trees.

Dismounting, both Archer and I took out our binoculars as we surveyed our home. My heart skipped a beat at what I saw. One of the garage doors was wide open. There was no doubt about it now. The Holy Joes had indeed come to the Station and had gained access to the building.

CHAPTER 22

With my worst fears now established that the Holy Joes had breached our home, our sanctuary, I quickly moved to saddle up on Ella. Archer turned and put his hand on my shoulder and stopped me, then he said, "Dixon, rushing in there and getting ourselves shot, will not help Alba. We do this like we have always done it before, we stop and observe. Look for anything that might give away that the Holy Joes have someone waiting in ambush for our arrival."

Once again, Archer was right. I was being reactionary to the events as they unfold, and that was sometimes not the best of ideas. I looked the older man in the eye and nodded an affirmative. He patted my shoulder in a fatherly gesture and added, "If Alba is still alive; we will find her. No matter what it takes."

"If she is dead?"

"Then we will find those responsible and send them straight to hell! No matter what it takes!"

Over the next 30 minutes, the sun inched its way upward, continuing on its arc of the day. The chill of the morning air was now starting to dissipate, as the dawn dew started evaporating on Rocky Mountain Arsenal prairie grass. After the half hour had passed, we had seen no movement, heard no sounds. It would seem as if the Station was abandoned.

Before mounting our horses, Archer and I checked our weapons once again. We did not arm Russ, nor did he ask for a gun. Having no experience with firearms, we were concerned he might accidentally shoot us.

Once we were contented, we were ready for battle, and that we could deliver any fight to anyone that was waiting to ambush us, we slowly moved out. We rode abreast of each other, but spread out, leaving 15 yards in-between us as we moved onto the Station. Archer was to the far west, Russ in the middle, and I was on the east. Ripley kept pace with Ella on my left side.

If any of the Holy Joes were in the building, waiting in ambush for our return, in the early morning dawn, there was no way that they could not have seen us on our approach. We rode out of the wildlife reserve's grass land onto what little pavement remained of Prairie Parkway, the road that was just north of the Station.

Just when I reached what was remaining of the fence enclosure around the old Commerce City Police parking lot, I saw a body lying by the open garage door. No more being cautious. I gave Ella some spur and loose reins as we flowed into a gallop. Behind me I heard Archer say, "Oh Shit!" as he did the same. Russ Papp followed and joined our charge to the Station.

Once reaching the body, I dismounted hastily, worried I had found Alba. Closer I got, I realized the body was too large to be Alba. In fact, it was a man. Bending down, I rolled the body over to get a better look, as Archer moved on into the garage, as if to cover me. Russ quickly joined me and in a matter-of-fact tone said, "That is Jim O'Toole. Not a nice man."

Not looking at Russ, I said, "Looks like Alba killed O'Toole when he breached the garage door."

Archer yelled out, "There is another dead hombre in here. Looks like our girl took down another one!"

Containing myself was no longer an option. I yelled, "Alba!" and then rushed headlong into the garage.

Heading toward the door that was the entrance to the station and partly sprung open, I kicked it hard. So hard that when it slammed open, one hinge gave way and broke. Moving into the interior, it was dark, the lights inside the Station had been extinguished. Not letting the darkness hamper my headlong rush to find Alba, with my EBR extended, I moved down the hallway towards our living quarters. In my rush and the almost total darkness I didn't see it, I didn't see the body lying crossways in the hallway, until it tripped me. Falling, I hit my head hard on the wall. Trying to blink away the flashes of light behind my eyes that were caused by my sudden stop as my noggin slammed into the wall, failed. Trying to gather my thoughts proved to be futile as my mind faded to black.

My eyes snapped open, and I jumped out of bed so fast, I became dizzy, and I stumbled crashing into Alba's and my bedside table. The sound of my awakening crash brought Archer, Ripley, and Russ running down the hallway. As soon as I gained my balance, I saw Archer standing in the doorway with Russ standing behind him. My head was hurting, and my heart was breaking when I asked, "Alba?"

"Dixon, she is not here!"

Pushing past Archer, I yelled, "Get out of my way!"

Archer and Russ stepped aside as Archer spoke. "We checked everywhere. Alba is not here."

I had to know. I had to search for myself. Between the 2 of them, Archer and Russ had gotten me into bed after I knocked myself out. I was such in a state of panic; I was not even embarrassed. Obviously Archer had gotten the lights back on. With Archer, Ripley and Russ trailing behind me, I began my frantic search of the Station. Each room had been ransacked. Clothes, dishes, chairs, all our items, had been gone through in a hurry. Reaching the security monitoring room, every monitor that I had spent months getting operational had been destroyed as if someone had taken a baseball bat to them. The pantry with the freeze-dried food had been ransacked, boxes torn open, packets of food thrown about, but for the most part, it seemed the biggest portion of the food was still here. The armory door was damaged, as if they had tried a crow bar on it, but it was still closed and intact, as the Holy Joes could not breach the door. I checked the bedrooms, showers, kitchen, ready room, exercise room, and our movie room. Just like my reoccurring dream, there was no Alba. Turning around, I shoved passed Archer, Russ, and Ripley. I made my way to the garage that we had turned into a barn. Alba was not there. Ella, Bonita, and Ladybird were all there in their respective stalls, unsaddled. Near the still open door were 4 bodies, all wearing the collars of the cleric, which told me they were all Holy Joes that Alba had killed. Alba had taken on the best of the best of the Holy Joes and had dispatched 4 of the attackers, but where the hell was, she?

I was frustrated, confused, worried sick, and pissed at myself for letting Alba down. Having searched the entire Station and realizing she was nowhere to be found, I sat down hard on the steps near the door in the horse stall area. My heart hurt. I was breathing hard. Having someone to love and then losing them was so much harder than not having that love for another at all.

Archer and Russ appeared on the dock. Russ went to the horses in their stalls and started the chore of feeding them, as Archer sat down on the steps next to me. Focusing on the old man that I had learned to trust and I said in a shallow voice, "Archer, I lost her.

Losing Alba is my fault. I should have never left her. This is all my fault!"

Archer, in a no-nonsense tone, said, "Dixon, knock it off! In all of this, you are missing what is truly important here."

I was stunned when Archer spoke. "Archer, what the hell are you talking about? What important item could I be missing in all of this?"

"In your mind, you have already jumped to the conclusion Alba is dead. Dixon, what truly is important here is that we never found her body. My guess Alba is not dead. They took her prisoner. If she is a prisoner of the Holy Joes, the only place they are going to take her is back to their compound in Brighton. Now, you listen to this old man, and you listen close. It is time to cowboy up. Struggles are real in this time of Tartarus, but to survive those struggles, stand up and take control, and, son, that is exactly what we are going to do. The Holy Joes done screwed with the wrong folks, the wrong clan. We are outgunned and out manned, but that is nothing new to us. We don't give a shit, and we are not arguing with them, nor are we going to negotiate with them. Once we get back to Brighton, we are going in with our guns blazing and we are taking Alba back. We are going to fight those sons of bitches. Dixon, the other important thing that you are missing is that the Holy Joes will be back here. They only took what they could carry this time around. They will be back for all the food, and something that they can use to breach the armory door. What they don't know is that there is a rocket-propelled grenade launcher and 6 rocket-propelled grenades in that armory. They don't have to come back and get them. We are going to deliver them to them. We are going to light that compound up! Joe Spawn wanted a war. We are going to give him a war!" My emotions ran the gauntlet between deep depression and acute anxiety. Archer had convinced me the most prudent thing to do was wait until morning to head back to Brighton and the Holy Joe compound. Worry and anxiety is like a rocking chair. It gives you something to do, but it doesn't get you very far. I had to calm down and rest up. Once we reached

Brighton, I would need all the strength and energy that I could muster.

We ate freeze-dried meals for our supper, then put together our cache of weapons that would make the trip to the Holy Joes compound. The prized weapon, of course, was the rocket-propelled grenade launcher and the 6 rocket-propelled grenades. I had never fired such a weapon, and we didn't have any extras for target practice. But Archer was familiar with the grenade launcher, and he would be the one using it.

Russ Papp seemed to be content having freeze dried food available, and he was eating his fill of it. Even though we had spoken to him about our attack on his old home to rescue Alba, I doubted he understood our objective and the destruction we were about to unleash. Archer and I would have to keep an eye on the youngster and gauge his reaction once we started our assault on the Holy Joes.

Ripley was saddened by the fact that Alba was not here at the Station. She continued to pace the Station in search of Alba. The dog had become more Alba's companion than mine since we had rescued her from the wild dogs. My sense was that Ripley understood more of what was going on than Russ Papp. She was hands down the smartest dog I had ever seen.

Surprisingly, I fell into a deep slumber once I laid my head down on the pillow in Alba's and my room. I had turned over on my side and I could still smell the essence of the woman I love. Knowing tomorrow would literally be a do or die day, I fell into a deep sleep.

After waking up just before dawn, the morning went by quickly. The biggest advantage of freeze-dried food was how quick you could make it edible. In no time at all, Archer, Russ, Ripley, and I had our breakfast. Since we had gone through and organized our weapons of choice for the assault on the Holy Joe compound last night, it was a simple matter of getting Ella,

Bonita, and Ladybird saddled for the trip north. We were loaded and had our butts planted in the saddle just as the eastern horizon was being painted with the orange and blue hue of a new day.

The sky was clear of clouds, but the air was crisp and cold and had a bite to it. I actually enjoyed mornings such as this, for it made me feel so alive. Long ago, I had learned a valuable life lesson. I had stopped acting as if life was a rehearsal. It was moments like this, sunrises like this, you learned to cherish them as if they were your last. The past and recent events were over and gone. Re-living them was not an option. Also, you needed to realize that the future was not guaranteed. Before we reined our horses north, Archer looked at both Russ and I as he said, "Even though we are now embarking on an assault to take down a religious compound, we must keep in mind that this religious compound, is a cult of zealots that have run amok. That Joseph Spawn is not a prophet, he is not God. He is like many in history, such as Jim Jones, Charles Manson, Marshall Applewhite, Shoko Asahara, Bhagwan Shree Rajneesh, and David Koresh, all which were exposed as false prophets."

As Archer had been speaking, he held a copy in his right hand of an official King James Holy Bible. He then opened up his bible and thumbed through it, looking for a passage. Once he found what he was looking for, he read to us. "The bible says in Matthew, 'For as the lightning cometh out of the east, and shineth even unto the west; so shall also the coming of the Son of man be.' The coming of the Lord for the judgment day shall be as swift as lightning that nobody will have time for any preparation and amendment."

Archer, after reading the passage, he looked towards the east into the rising sun and spoke as if he was speaking to God Ole Mighty himself when he said a prayer, "Ole' Lord give us the strength in this crusade, to rid this world of another false prophet, and bring our loved one home where she belongs."

Russ and I, in unison, said, "Amen."

CHAPTER 23

The trip back to Brighton was uneventful until we were halfway there. We were riding along Highway 85 north, next to my old neighborhood of Belle Creek, when Archer pulled back suddenly on his reins and brought his mare Ladybird to a halt. Russ and I followed suit and brought Ella and Bonita to a stop. I glanced at Ripley and her ears were standing straight up. Archer raised his hand to make sure we stayed silent, then he asked, "Do either of you hear that?"

It was obvious Ripley was hearing something, and so was Archer. Suddenly Ripley growled and then bolted westward towards the old forgotten carwash in what was left of the buildings in Belle Creek. Archer watched Ripley take off, and he asked, "Where the hell is she going?"

I still was not hearing what they heard, but I replied to Archer, "I know where she is going, and we need to follow as fast as we can."

There was no more discussion, and Archer, Russ, and I put some spur to the horses and the race was on following Ripley. Ripley, of course, was heading to the long tunnel type carwash that used to be called Tail Feathers. The same carwash I had used in the past to hide from a Gunner patrol. From previous experience, I knew it was large enough to house not only us, but the 3 horses.

Once we were tucked away and hidden in the carwash, and once the horses settle down, I could finally hear what Archer and Ripley had heard. In the distance, far away, was the distinctive "chuff, chuff, chuff" of the whirling blades of the air support helicopter of a Gunner patrol. Although distant, all of us could now hear the helicopter. It was difficult to determine in what direction the sound of the whirling blades of the helicopter was coming from. We all were looking through the plexiglass windows for any sign of a Gunner patrol. As much as we searched the surrounding sky and the roads next to Belle Creek, we saw nothing, no Humvees, no Gunners on foot, no helicopter. Wherever this patrol was, they were not close enough to have seen us. I was not sure if that was a good thing or not. They did not see us, and we did not know exactly where they were.

About 10 minutes after taking cover in the carwash, the distant sound of the helicopter faded away. It would seem that the Gunner patrol was moving away from our position. The problem with that was we had not located them and had no way of knowing if they were heading in the same direction that we were. We were already out gunned and out manned by the Holy Joes. We were ill-equipped to fight both the disciples of Joe Spawn and the Gunners.

Waiting another 20 minutes, I looked at Archer, and he shrugged his shoulders, then said, "We can't wait here all day. We got to move sooner than later. Might as well move now."

Leading the horses out of the carwash, we saddled up. Once again, we headed north towards the Holy Joe compound, but now we were keeping an extra eye on the sky.

It was noon when we turned east off of Highway 85 onto 136th Avenue. A half hour later, we made our way to the Berry Patch truck farm. This is where we had captured Russ Papp. We dismounted at the old abandon barn, which we had used previously. We decided to hunker down and make us some chow, and then wait for the cover of darkness before we moved on to the actual cult compound, which was, according to Russ Papp, about 2 miles away.

For the next couple of hours, we took care of Ella, Bonita, and Ladybird. We checked our weapons, and we put the feed bag on for us. We did not know when or even if we would have time to eat another meal.

Of all the hardships I had to face in my life, none was more punishing than this simple act of waiting for the darkness of the night. I closed my eyes, and I tried to envision Alba Jesse in my mind. My thoughts of her ran rampant through my thinker. All the good times, all the spats, we had. None of my thoughts were even remotely that she might be dead. I decided Archer was right. Alba was still alive. If they had killed her, I would have felt it within my bones. We were that connected. Thinking to myself, "Dixon Mateo, Alba and your unborn baby are out there waiting for you, counting on you to rescue them. Oh, how I loved this woman. I would save her or die in the attempt. No, if and buts." All these thoughts were ping ponging through my brains as I chambered a 7.62 x 51 mm NATO cartridge into my MK 14 Enhanced Battle Rifle.

Not sure when I had fallen asleep, but it was Archer that shook my shoulder waking me, and then he said, "Dixon, it is time to move on to Spawn's compound."

Having to blink my eyes several times to get my eyes adjusted to the darkness of the night. There was no campfire, and the sky had filled up with clouds, so the full moon above had a challenging time raining down any light onto the landscape.

Ripley had fallen asleep in my arms but was now wide awake and ready for what was to come.

After I stood and stretched the kinks out of my legs and arms, Archer spoke again, "Russ has the horses all saddled and ready to go. Not sure if he fully understands what is happening, but so far, he has been a trooper. Once we move on the compound to rescue Alba, we will have to monitor him. Not sure how he is going to react if we have to kill a few of those he knows."

Nodded my head with an acknowledgment, when I said, "Understood!"

A few minutes later, under the cover of nightfall, with Russ Papp now taking the lead, we followed in near silence towards the compound. I was out of my realm in this cloak and dagger approach. I had never intentionally meant to sneak up on someone and cause them harm. Until Alba had disappeared from the Station, I, for one in this world of Tartarus, was willing to live and let live. Only retaliating when attacked, but never stalking another. But for the Holy Joes to attack, kidnapped, or possibly have killed the woman I loved, I want to hurt those involved. I wanted them dead.

It didn't take long before Russ Papp brought Alba's mare, Bonita, to a halt. Archer and I moved up close to him when Russ whispered, "Just over that rise, you will see the Temple, the home of Reverend Spawn and the others, including my mother."

I was trying to look into Russ's eyes, to see if any understanding of what was going to happen was registering yet with the young man. If he fully realized what we were just about to do. The darkness of the night was preventing me from seeing

Russ's eyes. I was not getting any feeling one way or the other if Russ was comprehending his actions in leading us on this rescue attempt and war party against the home of his mother.

Archer just flat out asked the young ex-Holy Joe, "Russ, I need you to tell me you are okay with this. I need you to understand that some of these folks in the Temple compound may be killed as we try to take Dixon's wife back. Are you okay with that?"

Russ, still in a quiet voice, "Russ, Russ Papp understands that to save Alba that some others may be killed. Mr. Archer, they never liked me. I don't want to hurt them, but they hurt Alba."

Archer replied, "I guess that is the best answer I am going to get."

We all dismounted and Ella, Bonita, and Ladybird were trained enough we just dropped their reins, knowing they would not wander and if they did, they would come back with a quick whistle. Archer and I retrieved our binoculars and then Russ, Archer, Ripley, and I walked towards the rise to the east of us. Once at the bottom, we dropped, then crawled to the top, so as not to expose ourselves. Once we were at the top, we peeked our heads over and were surprised how close we were actually to the compound of Joseph Spawn and his disciples.

What we saw were 4 different buildings behind the razor wire and chain-link fence. The King Soopers shopping center was just how I remembered it as a kid. The smallest building was to the southeast of our position. Even in the darkness, I could see the unlit sign that said UPS store. The 2nd largest building in the compound was just north of the UPS building and north of our position and its unlit sign said it used to be an IHOP restaurant. Just seeing the old pancake restaurant building flooded me with memories of my childhood. It was always a wonderful treat to go there on a Sunday and eat breakfast with my folks before Tartarus ravaged the human species. The IHOP was the closest building, and that distance was 50 yards. There was a rectangular building east of the UPS store. The only sign left on the darkened building said T-Mobile, one of the old cell phone providers before Tartarus. North-east of the T-Mobile store was the largest building, and that was King Soopers, which at the time was one of the grocery store franchises in Colorado.

The clouds had drifted south on a slight wind, providing for now a cloudless sky above our heads and the Holy Joe compound. The full moon and the stars now provided us with enough light to see the guards that were manning the security fence in front of us. Within our eyesight, we saw 2 soldiers of the Holy Joes patrolling on the inside of the fence. They looked to be armed with Armalite M15 tactical rifles. These supposedly soldiers of God were carrying their rifles as if they knew how to use them.

As I was scanning the interior of the compound trying to memorize the layout, Archer had been scanning the western and closest perimeter to us to see how well it was defended. After several minutes, I heard Archer say quietly under his breath, "Shit! This rescue was already improbable, but now it might be damn near impossible."

Archer was looking to the north-west corner of the compound. Moving my field glasses in the same direction that Archer was fixated on and when my eyes finally adjusted to the dark, I saw it. But what was I seeing?

Archer quickly moved his binoculars to the south-west corner of the compound, and he whispered, "Oh shit! There is another one. I can't make out the far eastern corners of the compound in the dark, but I would bet you dollars to doughnuts they got one at each of those corners."

I was still looking at the north-west corner trying to figure out what Archer had seen. After a full minute, I gave up, and finally asked, "Archer, what the hell am I looking at?"

"Dixon, my boy, Joseph Spawn and his band of fanatics somehow have gotten their hands on some very heavy weaponry. What the Holy Joes have posted up in each corner of this nut cases compound are none other than Browning M2 50-caliber machine guns.

Browning 50-caliber machine was indeed a formidable opposition to overcome. Looking at Archer, "50-caliber or not, we are not leaving here without Alba."

Archer smiled, then said, "Totally in agreement, Dixon! This night is going to be one that you will be able to tell your grandchildren about. That is, if we live to tell the tale. First, we need to pick young Russ's brain on what is what in this compound. Once we come up with some sort of plan, we must keep the Holy Joes confused once our presence is known. The rocket-propelled grenades will help with that. These Holy Joes must not know what hit them and the lack of firepower we actually have. Keep the zealots guessing on what we are likely to do next!"

Archer patted Russ on the shoulder and asked, "Russ, my boy, tell me what is in each of those buildings and what we can expect."

Russ pointed at the old IHOP and said, "That is the cafeteria where everyone eats in shifts." He then pointed at what used to be the UPS store, then said, "That is where Reverend Spawn and his wives live."

Archer raised his hand and stopped Russ from speaking, and then he said, "The building that the Reverend lives in, does your mom live there as well?"

Russ nodded his head in acknowledgement before he answered, "Yes, she lives there."

Archer, looking at Russ, spoke again, "Dixon, and I have noted that the old UPS store is where your mom lives, and we will try not to create any type of ruckus there. No promises, but we will try not to."

Russ nodded his head slowly as if he was trying to understand, but I doubted if he was getting the meaning of what was going to happen. Archer was doing his best in a fatherly way to help Russ Papp comprehend, but I just didn't think it was all sinking into the young man. I could tell by the look on Archer's face he was worried about Russ, not in the sense that he would harm us or betray us and turn us over to the Holy Joes, he was worried like a father would worry about the safety and mental well-being of one of his kids. Archer patted the youngster on his shoulder and then said, "Okay, Russ, tell us about the other buildings."

Russ pointed at the T-Mobile store, and then said, "That is where they keep the guns and ammo on one side. And the other side is where they hold people to lock them up and to hurt them." Without skipping a beat, Russ continued his narration of the layout of the compound. "The big building Soopers is the Temple for worship service, and where Reverend Spawn does most of his talking."

Russ then pointed towards the far left and most northern part of the bigger building and said, "That is the barracks where everyone else sleeps."

Archer was silent and deep in thought, then he asked Russ, "Is there a way to sneak into the compound that you know about?"

Russ seemed confused by the question, then Archer added, "How do you walk out of the compound when you would leave?"

Russ pointed at the north-west corner where one of the 50-caliber machine guns placements was stationed, then he said, "There is a gate there that I walked in and out of."

Scanning the north-west corner with my field glasses again, I could see 2 men. But there was a tree in my line of sight, and there might have been more. I asked Russ, "How many men are usually at that gate?"

Russ said nothing, but he held up 4 fingers. A Browning M2 50-caliber machine guns and 4 men with Armalite M15 tactical rifles was an obstacle that would be hard to overcome. We could take them out with a rocket-propelled grenade and then breach the perimeter. But that would almost be certain death for us, since any element of surprise would have been lost just gaining access to the compound. Just like Archer had already mentioned, this rescue mission was already improbable, but now it might be damn near impossible. There had to be a way. None of us were leaving here without Alba.

Archer still looked in deep thought as he was scanning the compound with his binoculars. I asked him, "What now? What brilliant plan have you come up with?"

Archer pointed to the T-Mobile store and then said, "The best I got right at this moment is Russ says that building is where the Holy Joes hold people to lock them up and to hurt them. Thinking that is probably where they are holding Alba. Dixon, what do you think?"

"Makes sense to me."

Archer lowered his binoculars then rolled onto his back, "Then our objective is to take the T-Mobile store and their armory, which is next to it."

"Again, that makes sense to me. So, what is the plan to do that?"

Archer chuckled, "You mean without Russ, Alba, Ripley, you, and me, getting killed?"

"Ahhh, yeah, preferably!"

Archer then rolled to his side and looked me directly into my eyes when he said, "I have no friggin' idea!"

CHAPTER 24

Archer had no sooner stopped talking when we heard sporadic gunfire in the distance, on the far eastern side of the compound. Russ, Archer, and I peeked over the top of the rise and in the dark we could see flashes from many gun barrels light up the night. Then all hell broke loose. The whole eastern perimeter of the compound progressed into a full-fledged firefight. Some entity, someone, was attacking the Holy Joes on their eastern front.

Looking through my binoculars as the battle on the eastern perimeter escalated, I asked, "Who the hell are those guys?"

Archer quickly said, "I have not a clue, but they just gave us an edge to get Alba. This is total chaos, and it gives us an advantage to do what we need to do. But we must act quickly."

Archer then lowered his field glasses and pointed at the northwest-corner of the compound, where one 50-caliber machine gun was positioned. Then he said, "That is our entrance into the compound. Dixon, you take Ripley and Russ and head that way.

When you get within 40 yards from the entrance, take cover and wait."

"Wait for what?"

Archer smiled and patted the rocket-propelled grenade launcher, then said, "I'm going to blow that machine gun and those Holy Joes to hell in a handbasket. I am going to open up a hole in that fence for you."

Russ was not armed, but I had my MK 14 Enhanced Battle Rifle, and my side arm was my old fashion Uberti 45 long colt in a holster on my right thigh. Archer was right. This was our one and only chance to get Alba. I patted Russ on his shoulder, and I said, "Just follow me Russ, until we are inside the compound, then you take point as we move towards the T-Mobile store. Do you understand?"

Russ nodded his head as if he understood. I could only hope he would not slow me down once inside the Holy Joe compound. Russ and I stayed low as we started to move out, I had not taken 2 steps when Archer said, "Wait! Wait!"

"What?!?"

"Just a few pointers before you go. Here are a few rules of close combat. Number 1, anything worth shooting is worth shooting twice. Ammo is cheap. Life is expensive. Number 2, use cover or concealment as much as possible. The visible target should be in FRONT of your gun. Number 3, if you are not shooting, you should be communicating, reloading, and running. Number 4, if your shooting stance is good, you're probably not moving fast enough nor using cover correctly. Number 5, always cheat; always win. The only unfair fight is the one you lose."

The firefight on the eastern perimeter was still hot and heavy, and I almost laughed. "What? You could not have given me pointers like on the way here? Like when we had down time. Is that all I should know? Is there anything else you need to bring up at the last moment?"

Archer was thinking hard, then said, "There are more rules, but those are the most important ones. I can't think of anything else."

Almost laughing, I know that I probably rolled my eyes at Archer before turning back towards the compound when Archer said, "Wait! Wait, there is one other one you should know."

I turned to face Archer as he spoke, "Rule 6, the faster we finish the fight and rescue, the less we will get shot."

"Thinking rule 6 is a given."

Patting Russ on the shoulder, I said, "Let's hightail it out of here before he thinks of any more rules."

Ripley instinctively followed me, as I knew she would. Using the small rise and the trees as cover, we made our way to the north-west corner. I knew Archer was watching us with his binoculars. Once we were within 40 yards of the 50-caliber machine gun, I patted Russ on his shoulder and pointed towards the ground so we could hunker down and wait for Archer to take out the machine gun and open up the fence and razor wire.

The battle on the other side of the compound was not tapering off. In fact, it seemed to be more intense. The rat-a-tat-tat and the constant percussive sound of the machine guns on the other side were almost deafening. So thunderous I didn't hear the distinctive "chuff, chuff, chuff" of the whirling blades of the helicopter until it was almost on top of us. The chopper was now firing their 50-calibers down into the compound and even let loose an air-to-ground missile into the eastern perimeter fence. That cleared up the mystery. The Gunner patrol we had heard in the distance earlier today was for reasons of their own attacking the Holy Joe Compound. Just as that thought had cleared my mind, the very loud whoosh of the Archer Bowman fired rocket-propelled grenade went streaking not 5 feet over our heads towards the north-west corner of the compound.

There was a blinding flash of light when the rocket-propelled grenade exploded, filling the sky above the north-west corner of the compound with black smoke and falling debris. Raising my head, hoping not to be taken out by some detonated razor wire, I took a glance at the machine gun placement. From this vantage point, the Holy Joes were no longer on their feet and the 50-caliber seemed to be destroyed, but the fence was still intact. Archer must have seen this as well as the air above Russ and my head was filled with another propelled grenade. I ducked and covered Ripley again and waited for the almost immediate explosion. Another flash of light and even more smoldering black smoke and another round of falling debris. Keeping count in my head, I thought, "That is 2 rocket-propelled grenades out of 6." Raising my head again, it was obvious the 2nd grenade had the desired outcome, and a 10-foot stretch of chain-link fence and razor wire was gone, leaving a gaping hole in the security of the Holy Joe compound. Archer had created a backdoor into Joseph Spawns encampment. And it was time to use it.

Tapping Russ on his right shoulder, I had to yell above the raging gunfire on the eastern perimeter between the Gunners and the Holy Joes, "RUSS, TIME TO MOVE OUT!"

Russ or Ripley even hesitated as we moved swiftly, almost as one person, towards the hole in the fence. With my enhance battle rifle extended in a shooting position in front of me, using a motion threat scan of 360 degrees checking for hostiles and targets. Within 10 feet of the now destroyed machine gun placement, I saw the bodies of the 4 Holy Joes and 2 of them were still alive and moving. Remembering Archer's rules about close combat fighting, "Rule number 1, anything worth shooting is worth shooting twice. Ammo is cheap. Life is expensive." As I moved past the wounded and stunned Holy Joes, I fired 2 rounds into each of their chests.

Russ and Ripley moved up and stood just off to my right side, I had to yell again above the raging battle and chaos on the eastern side of the complex, "STAY CLOSE TO ME, WE ARE GOING TO MOVE TOWARDS THE T-MOBILE STORE TO FIND ALBA!"

Moving fast, and remembering another one of Archer's instructions, "Rule number 2, use cover or concealment as much as possible. The visible target should be in FRONT of your gun." Using as much cover as possible, Russ and I moved side-by-side south along the inside of the perimeter fence towards the old UPS store and T-Mobile building. It would seem that the Holy Joes for the most part had not realized that Russ and I had made our appearance into the compound. They were too busy battling the Gunners to the east of us.

The pilot of the Gunners gunship in his attack had been continuing, making round after round flying in a continuous loop from north to south and then south to north over the Holy Joes as we gained our backdoor entrance. The Gunners support helicopter had been raining down machine gunfire of their own on to the eastern Holy Joe perimeter until now.

It was apparent with the Gunner's helicopter, with its higher advantage from the sky must have noticed the rocket-propelled grenades that Archer had fired. The 2nd propelled grenade that had been set ablaze, probably had given the Gunners a location of the shooter, and the pilot looped his helicopter and was now headed westward to take on the new perceived threat. The "chuff, chuff, chuff" of the whirling blades was earsplitting as the helicopter was approaching our position.

Russ, Ripley and I had found an old junk car to hunker down behind, but we were not their intended target, and I doubted they even knew we were here. It was Archer that was their objective. Just as the Gunners helicopter was directly 60 yards above our heads, the pilot lowered the nose of the helicopter and fired 2 air-to-ground missiles at Archer. The missiles hit simultaneously in a fiery flash of light. My heart sank, as it was highly probable that Archer Bowman had been slaughtered in the Gunner's missile attack.

Archer's last position had been just due west of where Russ and I had taken cover behind the abandon car. We watched as a fire that had been ignited from the missile attack had taken hold and was rapidly spreading along the rise. I saw no movement, no sign of life. Russ had been watching as intently as I had been, and he shouted to be heard above the continuing explosions and automatic weapon fire of the battle that was still ongoing to the east of us. "Mr. Bowman, is he dead?"

Raising my voice to be heard, I said, "Not sure, Russ. One thing I know is that Archer Bowman is a tough old bird. Right now we have to concentrate on getting Alba, if she is still alive." What I didn't say was it did not look as if Archer had survived the Gunner helicopter attack.

Trying to put my worries about Archer aside for the moment, I needed to focus on the original mission of rescuing the woman I loved. There was one tremendous problem with moving onward towards the T-Mobile store. The Gunners helicopter was still doing flyovers checking for signs of life along the western perimeter fence. They were looking for Archer, and not Russ and me, since we were hidden from their view. But for us to advance on where we thought the Holy Joes might be holding Alba at, we would be exposed to the pilot of the gunship. We would not last 10 seconds out in the open against the machine guns and missiles of the Gunners' helicopter. For now, we were stuck right here. Could not advance, nor could we retreat.

Of all things, the Holy Joes gave us an option. Joseph Spawns men that were manning the Browning M2 50-caliber machine guns at the south-west corner of the cult compound got into the fight and opened up with their machine gun firing round after round at the invading Gunner helicopter, giving the pilot a new objective and target. Just as the helicopter spun in the sky to take on this new threat, there was a sudden flash from the rise to the west and 50 yards south of Archer's last known position. Archer had fired another rocket-propelled grenade, this time at the Gunner Helicopter. The propelled grenade only took a second to streak across the night sky before it exploded near the cockpit of the gunship. Through the black smoke and hellfire that was now spewing from the wounded helicopter, I watched the gunship spiral out of control towards the ground and then crash nose first into the IHOP restaurant. Not only was Archer Bowman still alive, but he had also taken out the Gunners' air superiority by destroying the Gunners' one and only helicopter.

The next thing that Archer did, I was not expecting. He must have known full well the 50-caliber machine gun at the south-west corner of the Spawns compound was also going to be an issue in taking back Alba. Archer fired 1, then quickly followed it up with a 2nd propelled grenade at the 4 Holy Joes manning the 50-caliber. Once I saw the streak of the 1st RPG, I yelled at Russ, "Duck! Duck!" Covering our heads again from raining debris of exploded body parts, machine gun, chain-link fence, and razor wire.

After the 2nd RPG explosion, there was a full minute of falling debris, waiting another 30 seconds, it felt safe enough to raise my head and look towards the south. Archer, just has he had at the north-west corner, had annihilated the south-west corner of the security fence of the compound. Keeping count in my head, Archer had fired 3 more rocket-propelled grenades, with the previous 2 that brought the count to 5. Archer had only one RPG left in his arsenal.

Remembering Archers rule of combat "Rule 6, the faster we finish the fight and rescue, the less we will get shot." I stood up and patted on Russ's shoulder to show we were moving. With my enhance battle rifle extended in a shooting position in front of me, using a motion threat scan of 360 degrees checking for hostiles and targets, with Russ by my side, we moved out towards the T-Mobile store and hopefully Alba.

CHAPTER 25

As Russ, Ripley, and I moved towards the IHOP building that had now been set ablaze by the helicopter crash, there was a plume of black smoke cascading into the night sky above the Holy Joe compound. The crackling and dancing flames had engulfed the building, just like the Gunner helicopter. We would have to skirt past the destroyed IHOP building to reach our destination, which was the T-Mobile store. The heat from the fire was scorching, and we had to keep a safe distance as we moved on past it, so our skin would not blister. I could smell burning and burnt wood, plastic, melting pavement, and seared flesh of humans that lingered in the air.

Uncertain of how many besides the helicopter pilot and crew had died inside that IHOP. I was not feeling remorseful for those killed in this battle. I was overcome with the futility of why, when humanity was almost wiped out by Tartarus, why the survivors continued to bring death and destruction upon ourselves. Human nature was not to be kind. We really were barely a step ahead of the animals that inhabit the earth. It truly was a dog-eat-dog world. In reality, it always had been.

Russ and I were alongside of the IHOP when I saw 2 charred bodies that had either crawled out of the fire or had been thrown out lying on what was left of the pavement. The body on the right moved its hand. I put 2 rounds from my battle enhance rifle into their chest. I was confused if I had shot the burnt man out of revenge or compassion. Trying to focus on the mission of rescuing Alba, I shoved the confusion and the horror of this battle into the dark corners of my mind.

With the Gunner helicopter taken out by Archer, I could hear better the keening and caterwauling sounds in the theatre of death of the eastern perimeter battle that was still ongoing. I was not sure who now had the upper hand, be it the Gunners or the Holy Joes, I didn't care. With both of our enemies now fully engaged with mutual destruction, it gave me a chance to sneak in the back door and hopefully save my wife and my unborn child. That was all that mattered.

Our movement south across the compound now took us away from the burning IHOP as we closed in on the T-Mobile store. The old UPS store was to our right. According to Russ, this was now the home of Joseph Spawn and his many wives, including Russ's mother.

Using a motion threat scan of 360 degrees, Russ, Ripley, and I moved closer to the T-Mobile store. With both hostile factions, Gunners and Holy Joes, still engaged on the eastern perimeter, we encounter no opposition once we came up to the old cell phone store. Once besides the building Russ, took over, and said, "Follow me, the entrance is this way." Russ pointed to the south.

Russ and I had our backs to the old cinder block wall that was on the west side of the building. We cautiously moved towards the south-west corner. Once we got to the corner, I thought since part of this building was the armory and Joseph Spawn cult members stashed their weapons here, that they must have some guards protecting the building. Bending down so I could look Ripley in the eye, I told her, "Ripley, I need you to check it out for us, to see if it is safe."

Ripley, understood, she always understood, and she slowly moved towards the corner, and just before she was about to turn it, Russ Papp said, "Let me check. If there is anyone there, I will know them. They won't shoot me."

"Are you sure?"

Russ took a second before he answered, "No, not sure, but Russ, Russ Papp, is not scared."

I pointed at Ripley and said, "Back up, girl, let Russ take the lead."

Ripley did as she was told, and she let Russ pass her and even with the battle raging and still engaged to the east of us. Russ Papp, the reluctant former Holy Joe, nonchalantly turned the south-west corner of the building. He could have not taken over 4 steps when someone, on the other side, yelled, with a man's voice, "HALT! IDENTIFY YOURSELF!!"

I can only imagine that the one that had yelled was now pointing some sort of weapon at Russ when he replied, "Harley, it is Russ, Russ Papp!"

Silence for a couple of tics of the second hand, then laughter. When the voice on the other side said, "Shit! Papp, you scared the crap out of Thomas and me. Where have you been hiding? What are you doing here?"

There were at least 2 guards, possibly more, but the laughter I had heard was from 2 distinctive voices, no more. Russ didn't even hesitate, nor did he lie, when he said, "I am trying to find a girl named Alba."

More laughter, "A girl? You're trying to find a girl in the middle of a firefight? You stupid twit, you wouldn't even know what to do with one if you found one. I should just shoot you for being the village idiot."

Not sure were the conversation between Russ and the 2 Holy Joe guards was going, but from the sounds of it, it was heading south. I bent down and touched Ripley and said just loud enough for her to hear, "NOW RIPLEY, NOW!" Ripley bolted around the south-west corner of the building, and I was just a step behind her as I turned the corner with my EBR rifle extended in front of me. Ripley's sudden appearance, then mine, had confused the 2 guards enough that they hesitated, not knowing how to respond. That momentary hesitation cost Harley and Thomas their lives, as I shot each one of them in the center of their chest. The one on the right stumbled, then I shot him again until he had fallen face first into the decaying pavement behind the cell phone store. Holy Joe, number 2 on the left, had already buckled to his knees, and I shot him in the head as I advanced towards their position. The head shot sprayed a fine red mist, followed by the distinctive coppery smell of blood. Once I was standing over the guards, I noticed the one on the right trying to sit up after being shot twice. I shot him a 3rd time in the temple. Both Holy Joe guards were now dead.

Lowering my rifle, I knew my savagery and brutality of killing the 2 Holy Joes might have rattled Russ, since he knew both of the men. He had not moved from the spot he had been standing in when I had turned the corner. I was not reading or getting a sense of his emotional state. Time was wasting, and I almost had to yell above the sounds of the continuing battle to the east of us, "Russ, are you okay?"

Russ's eyes were glued on the 2 dead men and said nothing. He might be in shock, but we didn't have any time to waste. Once again yelling above the resonating sounds of battle, "Russ, whatever you are feeling, you need to set it aside for now. We do not have time. Talk to me! Are you okay?"

Russ blinked his eyes rapidly, then moved his gaze up to look at me. After a few seconds, he said, "Yes, Russ, Russ Papp is okay."

There were 2 doors on this side of the building, the glass and metal original doors were no longer here. Someone had built some solid wood doors, and both doors had combination padlocks. I waved Russ over to stand by Ripley and me, and he moved cautiously towards me, still dazed by the killing of the 2 Holy Joes that he knew. Once he got besides me, I said, "It is okay Russ, you need to understand we are here to get my wife, and nothing, and I mean nothing, is going to stop me from doing that. Now tell me what you know about the inside of this building. Do you think there will be other guards? What side do they keep prisoners?" Russ pointed to the door on the west and said, "No, no more guards. No guards are on the inside. If Alba is here, she will be in there."

I pointed at the west door and asked Russ, "You don't know the combination, do you?"

Russ whiffed his head—no. In the distance, the battle on the eastern perimeter of the compound was dying down. Either both factions, the Gunners and Holy Joes, had sustained heavy losses, or one of them was fast becoming victorious. The constant rat-a-tat of machine gun fire had almost ceased and had been replaced by a single gunshot every few seconds. The victor of the battle was probably mopping up and killing the wounded of their enemy in a coup de grâce. Whoever the eventual victor was, I could not care less. Both were enemies in my eyes. All I knew was time was running out, and eventually someone was going to be looking for the armory and more weapons.

Ripley was prancing and spinning circles. Was she warning me about more Holy Joes or Gunners approaching, or did she catch a whiff of Alba? Pushing Russ back with my left hand, using the strap, I slung the enhanced battle rifle onto my back and then quick palmed my Uberti 45 Long Colt pistol and took aim at the lock and fired. The gunshot echoed this close to the building. Even though my shot penetrated the lock, it stayed closed. Taking aim once more, I fired once again at the lock. This time, the lock sprung opened and fell to the ground. Just before I was going to enter the building, 2 Holy Joe's dressed in the cleric collars rounded the south-east corner of the building and dropped to their knees and fired their rifles.

Spinning my body to face the new threat, at the same time firing my Uberti 45, I shot one of our new adversaries that was on the far right in the throat. But not before he shot me. I took the slug high up in my left shoulder. Stumbling backwards, I started to fall, as I fired off another round at the Holy Joe on the left and my bullet sailed over his head, missing him by several feet, just as he fired at me. Because of my stumble, mercifully, his bullet missed as well. I only had 2 shells left in my pistol and could not afford any more misses. Still in mid-fall, I fired again and this time I caught the uninjured Holy Joe in the center of his chest. The man wearing the cleric collar stumbled but did not go down, and he slowly raised his rifle to take another potshot at me when I fired the last remaining bullet in my Uberti. Reverend Joseph Spawn's disciple took the bullet dead center of his face, killing him instantaneously. I landed in a sitting position on my butt, slamming my back against the T-Mobile store wall as I watched the last remaining cult member gunman land rigidly on to his back. Both of Spawn's men were down and out of the fight.

Russ Papp, even though he was roughly in the crossfire between the Holy Joes and me during the gunfight, never took a hit. He was stunned by the ferocity of the hasty gunfight, but quickly came to his senses and bent down low over me and in a stuttering voice asked, "What can Russ do? What can Russ do?"

Ripley was spinning circles, not barking, but obviously agitated.

I needed to reload the Uberti, but my left arm was not having any part of that. The shock of being shot, and the sudden adrenaline rush had not worn off yet, and the pain had yet to initiate. But I could barely move my left hand and shoulder. I feared the bullet I took had done considerable damage. In a voice calmer than I truly was, I told Russ, "I need to reload. In my left pocket, there are shells for my pistol. My left arm is not working. Can you reload the Uberti for me?"

Russ looked worried, but he reached into my pocket and could retrieve some of the ammo there. He dropped several cartridges on the ground, but without having been told how, he was able to open the cylinder of the Uberti and, with some effort, could reload with 6 new shells. Closing the cylinder, he asked in a hurried voice, "What, what now, Dixon?"

Ripley still spinning, still not barking, but she was almost beside herself. She wanted to go into the old cell phone store, but was torn between doing so - or standing by my side. Reaching out with my right hand, I grasped Russ's left arm and said, "Russ, help me stand up!"

With considerable effort, Russ helped me to my feet. Leaning against the wall of the cell phone store, I took a deep breath. The pain of being shot was now making its appearance. I had to push through the pain. I still had not located Alba.

Now that I was standing, Ripley decided she wasn't needed anymore by my side, and she rushed through the now open door of the T-Mobile store. Once inside, the black German Shepard started barking up a storm.

Stepping away from the support of leaning against the wall, I hoped I would not fall. Finding my footing, then taking another deep breath, I once again grasped Russ's arm, and then said, "Russ, let's see what's got Ripley all rattled up."

Moving into the store, it was pitch black, but my eyes quickly adjusted to the low light and I could see Ripley barking and spinning circles in front of another locked door. I yelled, "ALBA!"

I could barely hear the muffled response from behind the locked door. "DIXON, OH MY GOD! I KNEW YOU WOULD COME FOR ME!"

I almost started to cry. Everything we had been through on this day now seemed more than worth it. We were far from being out of danger. We had to get Alba out of that room and far away from this place of madness as soon as possible. Stumbling forward with Russ's help, we moved towards Ripley and the locked door. Shouting so Alba could hear me, "STEP BACK BABE! I NEED TO BLOW THE LOCK OFF THE DOOR!"

Alba, from behind the door, responded, "I AM READY! GET ME OUT OF HERE!"

Once it again it took 2 rounds from the Uberti, but the lock finally blew open and fell to the ground. The door slammed open as Alba came flying through it and into my arms.

CHAPTER 26

I hugged Alba with my one good arm. I was so overwhelmed with emotion tears welled up in my eyes. Even in the dark interior of the old cell phone store, I could see that Alba was also crying. Hell, even Russ Papp was crying, and he didn't even know Alba. Alba let go of our hug, and both of her hands went to my face grabbing it, she brought my head down to her eye level and said, "Dixon, when the Holy Joes attacked the Station, I fought them the best I could and killed a few of them, but they over ran the Station and me. Thinking I was going to die. I was scared for the baby, and I was scared for you. I didn't want you to be alone."

Seeing and listening to Alba saying she was scared for me and the baby, and not herself, brought more tears to my eyes. How did I get so lucky to have crossed paths and then to fall in love with this courageous and unselfish angel? I had to know, so I asked, "Are you okay? I mean, really, okay? How is our baby?"

Alba, still holding my face in her hands, choked back the tears. Then she had a small smile, when she said. "I am good, Dixon, both of us are good! I can still feel the baby moving. He or she is a fighter, just like their father!"

Alba then leaned in close again and laid her head on my chest. She said, "I just want to hear your heartbeat. I need to know you are real and not an illusion."

"I am real baby, but we need to get moving. I do not know how many more hostiles are out there."

Ripley was still agitated, and spinning circles, but had ceased to bark.

Alba pushed back and said, "You're right, of course. But tell me what the hell is going on. There were no windows and all I could hear was machine gun fire, explosions, gunfire, and I think a helicopter."

"The Gunners with the helicopter for reasons unknown attacked the Holy Joe encampment. And Archer, Ripley, Russ, and I used their attack to sneak in the back door to locate you." Pointing at Russ Papp, I said, "Without young Russ here, we might not have found out where the Holy Joes were holding you at."

Alba turned to face Russ for the first time, then she moved towards him and pulled him in for a hug saying, "Young Russ, I have no idea who you are, or how you are involved in this, but it sounds as if I owe you everything, and I mean everything."

Russ didn't know how to respond to the sudden hug from a woman he had only heard about, but had never seen until this moment, and in an almost childlike voice, he said, "I love you, Miss Alba!"

Alba slowly separated from Russ and said in a bemused tone, "Believe me when I say I love you too Russ."

Alba then turned to me and cocked her head sideways in a bewildered way, as if she was trying to understand Russ's sentiment. I leaned in closer to her and said, "I will explain later. Just know Russ will be coming to live with us. Our baby needs an uncle."

Alba turned back to the ex-Holy Joe, and said, "Damn straight, our baby needs an uncle, and I think Russ is the perfect person for that job."

Even with all that had happened so far tonight, and with the outcome still uncertain Russ Papp after hearing Alba's welcoming declaration of bringing him into the family, our clan, put him on Cloud 9. The kid was all smiles, knowing he now had a family that wanted him. Knowing this rescue and catching up with the latest news was eating up valuable time, I said, "We need to move, before whoever the victorious faction is, be it the Gunners or the Holy Joes, that now control this compound, know we are here."

Alba, looked confused, and she said, "Wait, wait, and where is Archer?"

"Alba, I am not sure. Archer actually downed the helicopter at the beginning of the battle, but I have not seen him since then."

"Is he dead?!?"

"I don't think so. He might very well be dead, but the last I knew, he was alive. But for us to stay alive and try to locate him, we need to leave this place and get as far away as possible before dawn."

I handed my Uberti to Russ and said I need you to eject the 2 spent shells in the pistol and reload it, just like you did the last time. Russ still had a few 45 Long Colt shells from the last time when he loaded my pistol, so he took my gun and with a little more dexterity this time he started reloading the weapon.

Alba, confused, stepped back a few steps and now looked me over the best she could in the dark interior, realizing just now that for me to have Russ load the pistol, that there was something wrong with me. She saw my left arm was just dangling there, so she blurted out, "Oh my God Dixon, what is wrong with your arm?"

"I took a bullet high in my left shoulder, and now my left arm is near useless. Alba, you need to grab the enhanced battle rifle slung on my back. Russ is not very familiar with weapons, and since I can't handle the rifle with one arm, you need to take point when we exit the building. Once outside, I will guide you."

Alba wasn't having any of that. "First, we need to look at your wound and make sure the bleeding has stopped."

"NO! Babe, we don't have time. We need to move out now. You can doctor me once we are safe. No more discussion."

As Russ finished loading the Uberti pistol, he handed it back to me. Alba nodded her head in an affirmative, and said, "Understood, but at the first opportunity we get, I need to look at your shoulder."

"Deal, I promise you."

As Alba relieved me of the EBR rifle, Ripley crouched down low and stared at the exit door, and then started a long continuous low growl. Ripley sensed someone on the outside of the building. We were too late, I said, "Shit! Someone is out there!"

Just as I had finished speaking, a deep male voice from outside penetrated the darkness and in an eerie tone that echoed off the interior walls, said, "Unbelievers on the inside, drop your weapons, exit through the door slowly, and walk forth to be judged at the great white throne. This night shall be your judgement, by the Lord o' mighty!"

Although I already had a good idea, I asked, "Russ, who is that speaking?"

Russ stared at the door and said in a stutter said, "Reverend, Reverend, Spawn."

Looking at Alba, then back to Russ, I knew we were in a situation that was probably going to get all of us killed, right here, right now. During my hesitation on deciding what to do next, Joseph Spawn spoke again in that eerie and unnatural voice, "Understandable that right now you are wondering if you are going to live or die. Let me tell you what I know. You are the non-believer from the south that has killed so many of my clerics. Now searching for the woman from the south that we captured. You have twisted one of my flock, the slow child, named Russ Papp, to do your bidding. You also have a dog. I can smell the filthy animal from here. There are 8 clerics remaining. We were victorious in pushing back the other non-believers into the depths of hell. We are the chosen ones. I am the chosen one. Trust in the Lord with all your heart and lean not on your own understanding; in all your ways, you and the others must submit to him, submit to me, and I will make your paths straight. If you come out shooting, we will gun you down. If you try to wait us out, we will toss in a couple of hand grenades. You have exactly one minute to decide your fate. Surrender, or you will surely die."

Alba touched my arm and said, "The man is a self-indulgent, raving lunatic. He will kill us anyway."

"Probably, but maybe we have a slight advantage."

Alba asked, "Dixon, our situation looks bleak from my perspective. What slight advantage could we possibly have?"

"Archer! These nutcases don't know about Archer."

I had not convinced Alba, because she said, "We don't know if Archer is alive or dead. What makes you think he is still alive?"

"Same way I knew you were still alive. If you had died, I would have known it in my heart and soul. I knew you were still alive. Just like I know, Archer is still alive and is out there waiting to make a move. Remember, that old man is indestructible. Trust me on this. It is our only avenue out of this compound. We are going to surrender to Joseph Spawn, and buy us some time so Archer can make a move to free us."

Russ reached out and touched my arm. "Reverend, Reverend, Spawn will kill Ripley as soon as he sees her."

"I know, Russ, which is why Ripley will not hang around us when we surrender."

I bent down and pulled in the German Shepard, hugging her to my chest I patted her head. Pushing back from Ripley, she looked into my eyes. I spoke to her, "Ripley, as soon as we go out that door, you run, and you run fast. Go find Archer and bring him to us. Do you understand?"

Ripley's eyes never wavered from mine. Then she leaned in and licked my face. I knew she understood, she always understood. Joseph Spawn was getting impatient, and his voice echoed once again off the interior walls of the old cell phone store, "Whoever scorns Gods Will, my will, will pay for it, but whoever respects a command is rewarded. Unbeliever, what do you say? Shall you die in the dark huddled together or will you surrender to the chosen one?"

Alba said, "This guy's voice gives me the creeps."

Patting Ripley on the head one last time, I stood up and replied to Alba, "Oh, I bet his personality matches his voice."

Walking closer to the door, I yelled out to Joseph Spawn and what was left of the Holy Joes, "We are going to surrender. How do we do this without you shooting us as soon as we walk out the door?"

"Toss out your weapons and slowly walk out with your hands held high so we can see them."

"We only have 2 weapons, a pistol and a rifle." I nodded at Alba, who had the EBR rifle, and she reluctantly tossed the enhanced battle rifle out the door. I followed with tossing out the Uberti Long Colt pistol, which landed with a thud next to the rifle. Whispering to Alba, loud enough for Ripley to hear, "As soon as I walk outside, you release Ripley."

Alba nodded her understanding. I closed my eyes and said a silent prayer to the true Lord, and not this false prophet Spawn, that Archer was alive, and that Archer would come for us. Prayers said, I opened my eyes, and said out loud, "We are coming out."

With some considerable and painful effort and with a little help from Alba, I could raise my wounded left arm. Just as I cleared the doorway with my hands held high, as instructed, I felt Ripley brush past my leg as she bolted out the door and hopefully to freedom. By the time Joseph Spawn could react to Ripley hightailing it out of there, she had gotten a good 30 yards away to the west. Spawn yelled, "SHOOT THE DOG!" Three of the Holy Joes took aim and fired with their automatic weapons at Ripley fleeing, their bullets kicking up dirt and chunks of asphalt behind Ripley, never hitting her as she quickly disappeared through the gaping hole we had blown into the south-west corner of the compound. A few seconds later, she disappeared unharmed over the small rise to the west.

CHAPTER 27

The cult leader, Joseph Spawn, watched as Ripley disappeared into the darkness. Then he turned and looked at his so-called clerics with disgust. Ripley escaping had pissed him off, and hopefully Russ, Alba, and I didn't pay the price of that rage.

Alba and Russ had joined me on the exterior of the old cell phone store with their hands held high in surrender. Spawn had not fibbed, there including himself, were 8 Holy Joe's standing before us. Spawn was easy to identify. He was wearing a full, flowing white as snow robe made of what looked like gauze. At his waist was a red sash. Guessing the robe was his way of dressing like all the biblical renderings of Jesus one might see. Physically, he was not an imposing figure of a man. He was maybe 5'7" maximum and roughly 160 pounds. I was guessing he was 60 years old, with long brown hair with streaks of gray intermixed in it. His beard was also brown, streaked with gray. In his right hand, he held an automatic Sig Sauer P320 Compact pistol. And Spawn held the pistol as if he was more than familiar with the weapon. Before Tartarus wiped most of humanity from the face of the Earth, the Sig P320 was the pistol of choice of the

United States military. I could not help but wonder if that pistol was the same weapon that he had shot Russ's biological father with.

There was a familiar-looking woman who had to be in her late 30s standing just to the left of Joseph Spawn. The woman was dressed as Spawn was, with the white robe and red sash. She was small in stature, with long brown hair. She was actually quite beautiful. If I had just seen her wearing just the robe and the red sash, I would not have thought she would be dangerous. Her expression seemed to be soulless and that the fact she was holding an ArmaLite AR-15 in her hands told me different. This woman was very dangerous. Her familiarity was confusing me, as I tried to think about where I might have seen her before. Then I realized why she looked so familiar. Her facial features looked like Russ Papp. The more I thought about it, the more it convinced me this was Russ's mother and one of the many wives of Joseph Spawn.

The remaining 6 Holy Joes were all men wearing the distinctive collar of the clerics of old, all were in the 30s and 40s, and heavily armed with a mix bag of pistols and rifles.

The 8 that stood before Alba, Russ, and I had survived an all-out frontal attack by the ex-United States military, the ones I called the Gunners. Actually, they had defeated and or drove off the Gunners, like it or not, that was one impressive feat. The Holy Joes that had survived to still rule this compound were a hardened and daring group of survivors.

Spawn's voice, even outside the building, had an eerie, echoing quality. Alba was right. It was really creepy. He spoke to his disciples, "Bind them and put them on their knees."

As 3 of the Holy Joe men covered us with their automatic weapons, the others moved forward with short lengths of yellow nylon rope. Lowering my wounded left arm and shoulder was just as painful as when I had raised it. I almost passed out from the excruciating pain when the Holy Joe grabbed my arms and forced them behind my back to tie my hands. It was at this point I was wondering if I had made a huge mistake in not letting them murder us in a last ditch effort with a final gunfight. I had a feeling no matter what Spawn had in store for us would be a very painful death.

Once the 3 Holy Joes had Russ, Alba, and my hands tied, they then kicked the back of our knees, forcing us down. Alba had actually face-planted in front of her. Then one of them grabbed her by the hair and jerked her back so she was on her knees, like Russ and me. Rage flowed through my body seeing my wife and unborn child being treated in such a manner. I turned to look at the Holy Joe that had grabbed her hair and said, "If I ever get loose, you will be the first man I kill!" That prompted the Holy Joe to use his rifle butt to hit me in the face. I could feel bone and cartilage break as the blood gushed from my nose. Spawn spoke loudly, "ENOUGH! I want them alive!"

My body was already full of hate for these Holy Joes, given the chance, I would enjoy taking the life of every one of them. Looking to the west at the last places I saw Ripley and Archer, I said another silent prayer to the one only true God, hoping to save us from these lunatics in the form of Archer Bowman.

The sun was rising in the east to start a new day. With more sunlight, I now could see the scale of the carnage of the battle fought between the Gunners and the Holy Joes. There had to be more than a hundred corpses here and there throughout the compound. The effluvium of death was all around us. The battlefield had been baptized in blood and already the bitter, mordant perfume of corpses emanated and rode the slight breeze of morning.

Now that we were subdued and down on our knees, Joseph Spawn and the woman I thought to be Russ's mother, still holding their weapons, moved forward and stopped 15 feet in front of us. Spawn's flowing white robe made him look like a caricature of Jesus. Everything but the hiking boots he was wearing. The more I looked at the boots, the funnier it became to me, so I said, "Your Halloween costume of Jesus would be better suited if you wore sandals. Where are your sandals, Joe?"

The cult leader was quiet for half a minute just looking me over, before he spoke in that unnatural voice, "Unbeliever, God chose me after the rapture to rid this world of non-believers. It became my mission; the Bible is true, and I have become Christ. I am the tool to right the world, in the name of our Lord. Sandals, you ask? In my presence, you ask, where are my sandals? I warn you, from the world of darkness, I can set loose demons and devils in the power of scorpions and hounds of hell to torment you and the others. DO NOT MOCK ME!"

Joseph Spawn, the leader of his cult of clerics, was an absolute fruit loop. The most disturbing, most dangerous thing about Spawn was that he did not know he was mentally ill. And those standing next to him were just as nutty as he was to follow such a man. My eyes were looking directly up into Spawn's eyes. His pupils were dilated to the point that you could not see the color of his eyes. There was just a black circle smack dab in the middle of the whites of his eyes. I had no doubt that this man was doped up on something, be it a chemical drug, or just his own crazy notions. My gut instinct was now telling me that Joseph Spawn was Jim Jones, David Koresh, and Charles Manson, all rolled up into one man, one psychotic, that truly believed God had chosen him to do his bidding.

The blood was still flowing from my busted nose, but my mind now was in such a state that I felt no pain, be it my broken nose, or my shoulder wound, the only thing I felt was loathing for the man that now controlled Alba, my child, Russ, and my fate. I also started feeling some doubt. I had bet our lives on that Archer Bowman was still alive, now I was not so sure. Spawn was still looking directly into my eyes, as if he was searching my soul for answers to some question he only knew. I stared right back into his, never wavering, never blinking, when I said, "You know, Joe, you must suspect that you are insane, that you are nowhere close to being normal. I am baffled. Why so many stay here and have followed you? And hate to break it to you. You are not God; you are not Christ. You are a man just like me."

Spawn walked up close to me and then got on his own knees directly in front of me. He then did something that was so unexpected it almost unnerved me. He smiled, then he leaned forward and gently kissed me on my right cheek. Rocking backwards, still on his knees, still smiling, there was blood from my busted nose smeared on his lips. In that echoing, uncanny, and eerie voice, he asked, "Unbeliever, what is your name? What is your Christian name?"

I saw no reason not to tell him my name. And my thought was if Archer Bowman was still alive, I needed to keep Spawn talking long enough for Archer to get into position to hopefully mount some sort of retaliatory strike and rescue. I answered, sounding like Russ, "Dixon, Dixon Mateo is my name."

Spawn reached out and gently laid his hand on my shoulder, still with that unnerving smile and voice, he said, "Dixon, Those that follow me, which live under my guidance, remain here because I have thoroughly opened to them the seven seals. You think I am insane? Sanity is a small box; insanity is everything. I never thought I was normal, never tried to be normal. My disciples, know first-hand I am not normal. If the Bible is true, then I'm Christ. I realize I am as much the Devil as much as I am God. Those that survived need to understand that I am truly the most dangerous man in this new world of Tartarus after the rapture. Understand, Dixon Mateo, that before Tartarus, before the wrath of God, before the rapture, I was a man such as yourself. I was someone that nobody noticed, a tramp, a bum, a hobo, living in a boxcar with a jug of wine. The man you now see before you could also be a straight razor if someone got too close to me that I took a disliking to. I have no magical powers or take mystical trips, none of that kind of crap. Your eyes tell a tale. I feel it pulsate through your body. You think of me as some sort of hippie cult leader? I am here to tell you, Dixon Mateo, that you are wrong. I am the reflection of society before Tartarus, before the rapture. For that reason, and that reason only, I was the chosen one to do God's Will."

Joseph Spawn, with his eyes still locked on mine, stood up slowly. I was not sure how to respond to such ramblings of such an irrational and crazed mind. As I was rehashing the small sermon I had just heard in my mind, Joe turned his attention to Russ Papp. Russ met the unhinged cult leader's gaze and Russ's demeanor was one of strength as he looked towards the Reverend Spawn. I was proud of Russ for his stance and defiance of one that had controlled his life until a few days ago. After a full minute, Spawn spoke to Russ, "My boy, what am I supposed to do with you? It would seem that you brought this unbeliever, Dixon Mateo, to our doorstep. Your doorstep, your home. Have I not given you a home, food, a place to belong, after your father died? Haven't I become your father?"

Russ showed no anger, no emotions, and his simple mind unable to know what was really happening. He answered in the only way he could, with the truth. He said in a calm voice, "You are not my father. You shot and killed my father."

Spawn pointed at the woman in the flowing white robe and red sash. He then said, "Russ, I think your mother needs to address this issue. I think she has some questions for you. Honey, it would seem that our dear Russ has lost his way and seeks guidance. Can you come and speak to your son?"

My suspicions that the Holy Joe woman was, in fact, Russ's mom was now confirmed. The only surviving wife of Joseph Spawn walked forward, still holding her ArmaLite AR-15. Her face was expressionless as she stood next to her husband and the stepfather of Russ Papp, in a voice similar to Spawn's in tone and creepiness, she spoke to Russ, "How did you become to be with these unbelievers from the south?"

Russ, in his usual fashion of not being able to lie, "Mother, they captured me on the road."

"But yet, you seemed to help them. Why did you lead them here to our home?"

In his simple way, Russ spoke, "I live with them now. They treat me nice. I brought them here to get Alba. I didn't want Alba to be hurt, like all the others before." Russ was thinking hard, trying to be as truthful as only Russ could be, then he smiled and got excited, then added, "Oh, oh, and I get to be an uncle. Uncle Russ, Uncle Russ Papp!"

Russ's mother closed her eyes as if she was in pain for 30 seconds, then she opened them, and said, "All you have done is cause me misery, I wish you had died in the womb!" Russ Papp's mother then raised her rifle and pointed it at Russ, then shot her son in between the eyes.

CHAPTER 28

"NOOOOOOOOOOOOO!" I tried to stand. I was going to run the killer of Russ into the ground, but tied up and wounded as I was, all I accomplished was falling on my face. Two Holy Joes grabbed me by my shoulders and yanked backwards and put me back on my knees. The one that had broken my nose before took aim again with the butt of his rifle and slammed it into my face. More blood, more broken bones, but I didn't feel it. All I wanted to do was kill the bitch that had killed my friend Russ. If anyone in this world of Tartarus that was innocent of any wrongdoing, more deserving to live than anyone else, it had to be Russ Papp. I tried glaring at the mother that just committed filicide, but the flowing blood and the swelling of my face was now causing me to squint my eyes to focus.

The mother of Russ Papp showed no emotion, none, zero, nada, nothing at all with the murder and death of her son. She just stood there looking at her son bleed out laying at her feet. Joseph Spawn was no different. He pointed at me, then said in that echo chamber voice of his, "These nonbelievers entered our sanctuary, our temple, into a covenant not to seek the Lord, the God of their fathers. They came here uninvited, with malice in their hearts and their soul. Those that do not believe, that do not seek the Lord, the God of Israel, should be put to death, whether young or old, man or woman. These enemies of mine, who did not want me to reign over them, must die here, must die now, and slaughter them before me."

Russ Papp's mother took a step back into a shooting stance, raised the ArmaLite AR-15 to her shoulder, and took aim at Alba. Alba stared at her executioner and, with a powerful voice that never wavered, she said, "DIXON, I LOVE YOU! REMEMBER THAT!"

~

Just seconds before the woman wearing the white robe and red sash pulled the trigger, the distinctive whoosh of a rocket-propelled grenade filled the air above our heads. It exploded in a flash in the center of the Holy Joes. The explosion was so close to Alba and me we were flung backwards from the concussion wave that followed, and peppered us with flying debris of rocks, dirt, asphalt, and human remains. Still tied up, I rolled on my side and tried to clear my mind from the sudden explosion and shock wave of the propelled grenade. Lying in the dirt, I squinted through my swollen eyes to focus and the first thing I saw was Ripley running full out in our direction, followed by Archer at a full gallop on Ladybird. Archer had discarded the RPG firing tube after firing his last propelled grenade and had the reins of his horse in his mouth, and his rifle to his shoulder firing non-stop over the top of us. It would seem that Archer Bowman was alive and was coming to our rescue.

As my mind cleared some more, I remembered Alba, my sweet Alba. Scooting my hips and pumping my legs, I rolled over on my other side, hoping to locate Alba. She wasn't far. I almost rolled on top of her. The falling debris had peppered and covered her when the rocket-propelled grenade exploded. Focusing my eyes through the slits from the swelling of my face, my heart sank. Alba was unmoving.

Ripley got to us first, then followed by Archer on horseback, still shooting over the top of Alba and me. There was gunfire that was being returned from how many surviving Holy Joes I did not know. But Archer had put himself in harm's way to rescue Alba and me, as I knew he would.

Ripley jumped Alba's and my body and then placed her body between us and what remained of the Holy Joes. Barking up a storm, and protecting us, in the only way that she could.

Archer, in a classic move of a skilled horseman, dismounted and in almost the same motion bent down over us covering us with his rifle. Every few seconds he would fire his rifle at the Holy Joes, keeping them at bay. Archer still crouched over us, and using his rifle for cover fire, quickly produced an 8 inch buck knife, and as he was sawing through the rope, he asked, "Dixon, you look like shit! How bad are you?"

"The Holy Joes beat the crap out of me. My eyes are swelled to the point I can't see very well, and I got shot in my left arm. Can't handle a rifle, but if you got a spare pistol, I could do that."

Once freed from the rope, Archer produced a full auto Glock 18 from a holster on his right hip. Handing the pistol to me, he said, "Put it in semi-auto, we need to conserve ammo. How is our girl?"

Clicking the Glock into semi-auto mode, I leaned over and placed my head on Alba's chest. Thank the true Lord. She was breathing. I quickly checked for any wounds that may have come from the shrapnel of the grenade. Seeing none, I said, "She is breathing, thinking she just got knocked out from the concussion of the grenade."

Archer raised his eyebrows. "My grenade?"

"Yes, your grenade!"

Archer took one look at the dead body of Russ Papp, and as a tear formed in his eye, he asked, "Who shot the boy?"

"His mother! The one wearing the white robe and red sash!"

Another volley of bullets from the remaining Holy Joes was kicking up dirt, asphalt, and ricocheting every which way, reminded us we were still vulnerable where we were. Archer fired his rifle twice to keep the remaining Joes ducking their heads, then he grabbed Alba and dragged her into the old cell phone building out of the line of fire. Ripley and I swiftly followed. Once in relative safety for now, I checked Alba's pulse, and it was strong. She was just out like a light. Feeling a tad better about the woman I loved, and our baby's survival, I asked Archer, "How many Holy Joes are left?"

"Only 3, the man wearing a white robe, Russ's mother, and one other man. The other 5 got splattered with the grenade. We got a problem, though. I am about out of ammo."

Explaining, "The man wearing the white robe is none other than Joseph Spawn himself." Pointing at the interior door that separated where the Holy Joes had been holding Alba, and the rest of the strip mall, I said, "According to Russ, on the other side of that door was the Holy Joe's armory."

I stepped up to the padlock on the door and set the Glock 18 into full auto and fired. The lock blew apart and thudded to the floor. Now that the sun had risen, it was still dark in the interior, but our eyes adjusted, and we could see fairly well. Pointing towards the door to the exterior, I told Ripley, "Guard that door, girl, let us know if anyone is coming."

Ripley barked once, letting me know she understood. She always understood. As Ripley headed to guard the door, Archer and I went into the Holy Joe armory.

Joseph Spawn's disciples had gathered an impressive armory. Archer discarded his near empty rifle and went shopping. Bowman found and decided on an MK 14 Enhanced Battle Rifle, just like the one I had to surrender today, then he quickly loaded it with 7.62×51mm NATO cartridges. Archer then located the same exact pistol he had handed to me, another full auto Glock 18. He loaded the 9MM magazine, then found 3 more magazines and quickly loaded them. He then he took my Glock and made sure it was fully loaded, then handed me 2 more fully loaded magazines. Walking back into the side of the building that Alba and Ripley were, we noticed that Alba had woken up, well, sort of, and had gotten herself into a sitting position. Ripley, with her nose pointed towards the exterior door as instructed, had moved close to Alba to protect her from any intruders.

All gunfire had ceased on the exterior of the building. Leaning down, I asked, "Alba, how are you feeling?" Still groggy, she replied, "Feel like I got hit by a truck."

Gently touching her face, I said, "You feel that way from the concussion wave of a rocket-propelled grenade that Archer fired in our direction."

Alba, still dazed, raised her eyebrows and asked, "A grenade that Archer fired at us?"

Archer interjected, "Ahhh, yes, sorry about that!"

Still touching my lover's face, I added, "Babe, believe it or not, for now it had saved our lives."

Archer leaned down and looked into Alba's eyes as he handed her a loaded 9 mm Beretta APX Centurion semi-auto pistol. He said, "Keep this close until Dixon and I return. Anyone else walks through that door, you shoot them!"

Alba took the Beretta, and then put a shell into the firing chamber, as she spoke, "Understood. Where are the 2 of you going?"

Alba was still dazed, her left eye was dilated, and her right eye was not, and I was concerned that she had a concussion. I told her, "There are 3 Holy Joes left, including Joseph Spawn, Russ's mother, and one other man. Archer and I are going to finish this once and for all. We are going hunting!"

CHAPTER 29

Alba said, "The hell you are! Not without me!"

Alba tried to stand, but she lost her balance and fell hard back to her butt. Bending over Alba, I gently grabbed her chin and brought it upwards as I gently kissed her on the lips. After kissing this woman that had stolen my heart, I could see that her pupils were still out of whack. One eye was dilated, and the other was not dilated at all. In the most assuring tone that I could muster, I said, "Babe, I think you have a concussion, and right now, I need you. Archer needs you to stay put, and we need to protect our family, and our family to be. That baby you are carrying is part of both of us, and they have already put you and our child through a gauntlet that most would have succumbed to. You are done fighting our enemies for now. We cannot put you and the baby through any more stress than you have already endured. I love you, Alba, and I love our child more than anything else in this world. You need to sit the rest of this battle out and let Archer and I finish this."

Alba looked me straight in the eyes and, by the tears that had formed in her eyes, she knew I was right. She gently touched her belly and said, "How can someone so little - touch so many hearts?"

I reached down and pressed my hand to Alba's belly to feel the baby, and I felt as if a bolt of lightning had hit me. I felt electrified. In my mind, the darkened room was flooded with an all-knowing bright light from above. A vision or prophecy of what was to come hit me. Suddenly, my mind was now focused, and it all became abundantly clear. In that moment that lasted less than a tic-tic of a minute, I saw the future. The prophecy or dream was a map. A map of what will be. In the past, I had always had a sketchy relationship with God. A believer, but God had never spoken to me before, until this very moment. The visions that had flashed through my mind were like a newsreel of events and memories not yet lived. I saw our child, our son, as he was born. In blinding flashes, I saw our son grow into a man of stature, a leader of other distinguished men. Alba and my flesh and blood, our son, was the one, the chosen one, to bring humanity out of the dark ages of Tartarus back into the grace of God and bring the human species back into balance with nature. Everything that had happened prior to this instant was the foundation of a better world, a better humanity. This moment in all the madness, in this battle, in all the chaos, in this world of Tartarus, seemed to make it all worthwhile somehow. God had a plan, and it didn't favor false prophets such as Joseph Spawn. The one and only true God had flushed the human race of those that were not worthy. God favored those that would inherit the earth. God favored Alba and my child, like no other. The vision I had just experienced was etched into my mind, my soul, and it was true. This I knew in my heart. Leaning in closer, I whispered to Alba, "I know why, and now I know the purpose. God just spoke to me."

Alba had placed her hand on top of mine when I touched her belly. After I had spoken, a smile crossed her face, and as she gave my hand a slight squeeze, she said, "I saw it as well. I experienced what you saw. I am overwhelmed with relief, and with love."

Tears formed and streaked down my cheeks when I asked, "Then I am not crazy? I have not lost my mind?"

"No Dixon, I saw it too! You are not crazy!"

Archer had been standing behind me, finally brought Alba and me back to the reality of the situation. He said, "Not sure what you both think you saw, but we need to finish this fight with Spawn and that bitch of his. We need to do it now!"

Alba nodded her head in understanding as I stood up and faced Archer, then said, "Let's do it! Let's finish this!"

Archer quickly reloaded his enhanced battle rifle. Even though the adrenaline rush of close combat had numbed the pain from my broken face and wounded left arm, I still could not handle a rifle because of my injuries. Archer made sure my Glock 18 was reloaded. He then stuffed several loaded magazines in my pockets. Once that was done, I asked, "How do we play this?"

Archer smiled, and replied, "I have no idea! I say we sic Ripley on them, and as soon as she has cleared the door, I will go first covering to the right, then you follow covering the left."

"Sounds chaotic."

Archer laughed out loud, then said, "No shit! You got a better plan?"

"Nope!"

I realized the vision I saw showed Alba and our son surviving this battle. It didn't show Archer, Ripley, or me living to tell the tale. I guess it didn't matter. All that was important is that Alba and the baby live. Taking a deep breath, I asked Archer, "Are you ready?"

Archer said nothing, he just nodded his head in an affirmative. Ripley had been spinning circles in the close confines of the building and was eager to be given a command, so I did. "Ripley! Go! Go!"

Ripley bolted out the door and drew rapid fire from the right. Whoever was shooting at Ripley had not considered how fast the German Shepard was. Dirt, asphalt, and dust were kicking up behind Ripley, as she was the diversion we needed to exit the building. Archer, in a shooting stance with the enhanced battle rifle extended in front of him, moved through the doorway into the daylight. He immediately began firing to our right. Although wounded, I followed, scanning the Glock to the left as soon as I stepped over the threshold. There was no threat visible in front of me, and in just a matter of a few seconds Archer had quit firing the EBR and said in a loud voice, "Scratch one Holy Joe!"

With no threat to the left, I glanced to the right and saw the Joseph Spawn disciple that had been wearing the cleric collar had been killed by Archer. When Ripley had made her dash out the door, it had been in a straight line. Giving the distraction Archer needed to kill the Holy Joe before he could focus in on us as we exited the building. Ripley had run full out, then circled into a 360, and was now coming up behind Spawn's dead soldier. Once she reached the body, she squatted and peed on the man's head. Archer chuckled and said, "Seems like a fitting 'howdy do' and a proper send off from Ripley."

The swelling and my broken face prevented me from smiling, but Ripley's reaction did somehow seem fitting for the events of the day. Archer's smile faded as he knew we had not yet completed our mission. He then said, "We still got to find Spawn and his wife. Since I have more firepower with the EBR, I will take point. Dixon, you need to bring up the rear guard. How are you doing? Are you up to this?"

"Beat to hell, but functional. I got your back."

"Dixon, you are a tough SOB and a good man. Let's move out!"

With Ripley to the left of Archer and me, we turned the southwest corner of the old T-Mobile store. Now we could see the entire Holy Joe compound, or rather what was left of it. The fire that had started when Archer had downed the Gunners' helicopter had now engulfed all the buildings except the T-Mobile store. There was black billowing smoke above the compound with ashes carried on the wind raining down on us. What we saw before was a total chaos of war. In-between the burning buildings, the ground was littered with the dead of both Holy Joes and Gunners. The carnage before us was in some aspects biblical, and in some ways it showed the ultimate destruction of humanity. Maybe this battle was the battle to end all wars. Even with this combats devastation and butchery, it gave me, us, what we long for in life, in this world of Tartarus. The vision that Alba and I had experienced gave us purpose, meaning, a reason for living. I knew at this very moment that this battle had to happen for our son to thrive and become the leader that God and humanity needed. To bring forth from the ashes a new world, a new beginning. Archer yelled out, and pointed, "Got them! Spawn and the woman are both on horseback to the north!"

Just as Spawn and his wife we getting ready to spur their horses into a gallop, Archer laid the enhanced battle rifle on the hood of an old Ford F250. Now the EBR had a stabilized shooting platform. Archer took his time aiming, then he gently squeezed the trigger. Archer's bullet hit Joseph Spawn dead center in his chest. As the cult leader slumped in his saddle, Archer squeezed off another round, catching Spawn in the head, dropping him like a sack of potatoes dead to the ground. His wife and the killer of her only son, Russ, reined her horse in a circle around Joseph Spawn's body. Once realizing her man was dead, she spurred her horse into a full gallop northward. I said, "She is done for. Let her go."

Archer didn't even look at me. "Nope, she killed Russ!" He then fired again, knocking the last surviving Holy Joe from her horse. Russ's mother hit the ground hard, but she immediately sat up, giving Archer another target as he shot her in the head. Archer slowly stood up straight and turned to face me as he said in a resolved tone, "Now she is done!"

EPILOGUE:

It took almost 6 months. But, our home, the Station, had been restored to even a better condition that it had been into before the Holy Joes had attacked it and had kidnapped Alba. The birth and delivery had gone well, and Alba had been a champ, and our son was healthy and was thriving. When Alba went into labor and the delivery started, Archer was an emotional wreck and had to leave the room before the baby was born. It was like he was the expectant father and not just the adopted grandpa. For someone that was tough as nails, and more capable than any man I had ever known before, his distress over the birth made me laugh. It would seem watching his adopted grandson being born had been more than he could bear. He told Alba, "Sorry, I can't do this. I am about ready to cry. I am going to go tend to the horses before someone revokes my man card." Archer Bowman, took Ripley, and they then both bolted out the door.

Several hours later, our son was born. He was beautiful. I used a fishing scale liberated from the abandon Walmart and weighed him. A whopping 8 pounds and 7 ounces. He was a big boy, with a full head of dark hair already. After Alba nursed the youngster, she said, "You better take him and show Archer and Ripley, so both know everything is okay. I know how worried they were."

I was all smiles, and feeling peaceful, when I gingerly scooped up our son. Making sure he was wrapped up tight in a fresh blanket, I leaned in and kissed Alba, like lovers do. I knew Archer and Ripley would be pleased, as I headed out the door to find them.

I found both Archer and Ripley sitting down watching the sunset on the western horizon as the horses grazed in front of the Station. When Archer heard me, he turned and his face split into a huge smile, "I take it, everyone is okay?"

As I sat down next to Archer, I handed him the baby, and said, "Better than okay. Meet your new grandson."

Ripley laid her head gently in my lap, with her eyes never wavering from looking at the newborn, as I handed over the new addition to our clan to Archer. Ripley the protector of us all seemed at peace with knowing she had another to love and to protect.

Archer took the baby and held him like he was unfamiliar with such things, but he quickly got the hang of it as he drew the boy into a loving embrace. After a few minutes of staring at the baby, Archer spoke. "When Alba and you said that you had a vision from God about this little guy, I was skeptical. Now that I am holding him, I feel it as well. There is an aura around this child of goodness, and I feel the power that resonates with him. He is everything you said, and the prophecy you saw will be fulfilled. Looking at him now, I know in my heart and soul, he is the new beginning of all things: wonders, hopes, and new possibilities. I will teach this boy everything I know, and I am sure he will teach me a few things. What is his name?"

I reached out and touched Archer on the shoulder and said, "I thought you would never ask. His name is Russ Archer Mateo."

Archer looked at me and he was speechless for a few seconds, then the tears rolled down his face. He struggled for the words. "I am deeply honored, and I know Russ would have been delighted with the name."

The End – For now!

Kurt James

211

AUTHOR'S NOTE:

If you, the reader, has made it this far, that means you have finished reading my dystopian adventure, and I would just like to take a line or two to thank you for purchasing my work, and I hope you enjoyed the book.

It is my hope you have found setting of the state of Colorado to be a living and breathing character as much as Dixon, Alba, Russ, Archer and Ripley. I love Colorado and everything it offers.

I also wanted to assure you that the Colorado geography, described in the story between Commerce City and Brighton, Colorado, does in fact exist. Every road, highway, and Belle Creek which I currently live.

I wanted folks who were locals or familiar with this Colorado area to be able to follow along on this future adventure more easily in their mind and to be able to travel if they wanted to on horseback, foot, or even by car or 4 wheel drive the same path of Dixon, Alba, Russ, Archer in their quest of surviving in a world on the brink of extinction.

KURT JAMES BIBLIOGRAPHY

ROCKY MOUNTAIN SERIES
Book 1 – Rocky Mountain Reckoning (Download or Paperback)
Book 2 – Rocky Mountain Retribution (Download or Paperback)
Book 3 – Rocky Mountain Ghost (Download or Paperback)
Book 4 – Connor's Saga (Download or Paperback)
Book 5 - The Keegan Trail (Download or Paperback)
Book 6 – Rocky Mountain Moonshiner (Download, Paperback, and Kindle Vella)
Book 7 – Raphael Eye for an Eye **(COMING SOON!)**

GRAND COUNTY SERIES
Book 1 – The Daunting (Download or Paperback)
Book 2 – When the Song Vanishes (Download or Paperback)

PATTON – BOUNTY HUNTER SHORT STORY SERIES
Adventure 1 – Patton – Bounty Hunter (Download Only)
Adventure 2 – Patton – Bounty Hunter (Download Only)
Adventure 3 – Patton – Bounty Hunter (Download Only)
Adventure 4 – Patton – Bounty Hunter (Download Only)
Adventure 5 – Patton – Bounty Hunter (Download Only)
Adventure 6 – Patton – Bounty Hunter (Download Only)
Adventure 7 – Patton – Bounty Hunter (Download Only)
Adventure 8 – Patton – Bounty Hunter (Download Only)

PATTON – BOUNTY HUNTER Short story collection 1
Adventures 1-7 (Download or Paperback)

Wandering Man Series (Poetry)
Poetry and Thoughts of a Wandering Man (Download or Paperback)
Poetry and Reflections of a Wandering Man (Download or Paperback)

OTHER BS SERIES
Colorado Ghost Towns, Hauntings, Treasure Tales, and Other BS (Download or Paperback)
Kansas Ghost Towns, Hauntings, Treasure Tales, and Other BS **(COMING SOON!!)**
Wyoming Ghost Towns, Hauntings, Treasure Tales, and Other BS (Download or Paperback)
Old West Lingo, Wisdom, and Other BS (Download or Paperback)
Corny Cowboy Jokes, Ponders, and Other BS (Download or Paperback)

The Tartarus Variant - Book 1 - (Download – June 2023, Paperback – June 2023, and Kindle Vella)

Devils Tower - The Spirit of Chiha Tanka **(COMING SOON!)**

ABOUT THE AUTHOR

Kurt James was born and raised in the foothills of the Colorado Rocky Mountains. With family roots in western Kansas and having lived in South Dakota for 20 years Kurt naturally had become an old western and nature enthusiast. Over the years Kurt has become one of Colorado's prominent nature photographer's through his brand name of Midnight Wind Photography. His poetry has been featured in the Denver Post, PM Magazine and on 9NEWS in Denver, Colorado. Kurt is also a feature writer for HubPages and Creative Exiles with the article's focused on Colorado history, ghost towns, outlaws, and poetry. Inspired at a young age by writers such as Jack London, Edgar Rice Burroughs, H.G. Wells, Louis L'Amour and Max Brand have formed Kurt's natural ability as a storyteller. Kurt has published 15 books.

Made in the USA
Thornton, CO
07/06/23 10:47:41